# THE BOY WHO MET a WHALE

# THE BOY WHO MET a WHALE

## NIZRANA FAROOK

PEACHTREE
ATLANTA

Published by
PEACHTREE PUBLISHING COMPANY INC.
1700 Chattahoochee Avenue
Atlanta, Georgia 30318-2112
*PeachtreeBooks.com*

Text © 2021 by Nizrana Farook
Cover image © 2021 by David Dean

First published in Great Britain in 2021 by Nosy Crow Ltd.
The Crow's Nest, 14 Baden Place
Crosby Row, London SE1 1YW

First United States version published in 2022 by Peachtree Publishing
Company Inc.

Composition by Lily Steele

Printed in the United States of America in July 2021 by Lakeside Book
Company in Harrisonburg, VA
10 9 8 7 6 5 4 3 2 1
First Edition
ISBN: 978-1-68263-373-1

Cataloging-in-Publication Data is available from the Library of Congress

*To the Maalus of my life,*
*who've been there for me*
*not just in sunshine, but also in storm*

# Chapter One

The boy clung to the rail with a death grip as the ship lurched violently in the storm.

It was sinking.

All around him was darkness and the roar and crash of waves as the ship buckled and rain lashed down. The wind was shrill and whip-sharp. But for all the noise, the ship was empty of people. Where was everyone? The boy ran along the deck, slipping and sliding to the wheelhouse.

It was deserted.

He sprinted down the length of the ship, hurtling below deck to the captain's quarters. He pounded on the door, desperate to be heard over the sound of the thunder and the howling of the wind. But it was impossible.

The door opened suddenly and the first mate slipped out, a long leather pouch clutched in his hand. He startled when he saw the boy, and quickly hid his hand behind him.

"Sir, the storm—" began the boy, but the man shoved him aside and hurried down the passage.

The boy held on to the side for balance and stumbled into the cabin. The captain was lying in his bunk, fast asleep. The room had been ransacked: drawers were hanging open and books had been tossed all over the place. The ship listed sharply and the debris on the floor slid to one side of the room where water was pooling, creeping darkly over fallen books.

The boy froze in shock. The crew had *known* they would be sailing into a storm. Why was the captain asleep so soundly? Why was the *whole ship* asleep? Apart from…

He stormed out of the captain's cabin and scrambled up to the deck. A lifeboat had been lowered into the sea, and the first mate was getting ready to climb down, accompanied by a man the boy recognized as the ship's cook.

He stared at the men, a cold fear clamping around his heart as the rain soaked through him. "Marco!" he screamed. "What did you do? Did you *drug* them?"

The first mate looked back and shrugged, not even bothering to deny it.

Rain pelted the men as they prepared to get in the boat. Something snapped in the boy, and he raced toward them and plucked the leather pouch from the first mate's pocket.

Yelling, the men gave chase as the boy sprinted away down the ship. Lightning lit up his running figure. The ship groaned and shifted. The men stumbled and one fell as the boy doubled back, jumping over the fallen man and speeding past his furious companion. The first mate took out a knife that flashed silver in the gloom of the night. He ran fast, closing in on the boy as water filled the deck and crept up his ankles.

It was over. The ship was going down, and it was too late to save anyone. The boy wailed in anguish as he threw himself over the side and into the lifeboat. The ship tilted and groaned, making a huge cracking sound as it broke apart. The men ran to the railing and yelled at the boy, but the rain blotted out everything as he rowed swiftly away. The last he saw of the ship was it careening jerkily off course.

The boy screamed into the wind and wept for his lost friends.

# Chapter Two

The baby turtle scuttled down the golden beach, wet and gritty with sand. Bit by bit scores of others emerged, their shiny black bodies, flailing limbs, and beady eyes glinting in the early-morning sun. They scampered toward the water, their little legs scuffling over the freshly turned-up sand. A bale of tiny turtles—all eager to make their first meeting with the sea.

Razi laughed as he ran after them, careful not to step on any of the little creatures. The sight never failed to amaze him and lift his spirits. He'd seen it a hundred times, coming early to this stretch of beach to watch the newly hatched turtles running into the sea at sunrise. There was a white one among them, an albino turtle, the pattern on its back etched out in shiny black lines. It was lagging behind and in danger of getting lost.

"Go on! Go, your friends are leaving!" called Razi. He knew not to touch it and so he hoped his voice would cheer it on instead. Sure enough, the white turtle perked up and scuttled after the others.

Overhead a yellow-beaked ibis wheeled past. Razi kept an eye on it in case it tried to attack the babies.

The sea was a grayish blue, deepening gradually to a brilliant turquoise with the rising sun shining on the waves. Coconut trees fringed the beach, their wiry trunks twisted like swaying cobras.

Standing on the shoreline, Razi watched in awe. A wave came in, drenching the baby turtles as they swarmed up to meet it. They hopped into the water, greeting it playfully. Razi held his breath. This part always worried him. The turtles looked so little and fragile. But the whole lot of them swam away happily, dots of black on the rolling blue waves surging into the great ocean.

He sat cross-legged on the sand and watched them bob away. They disappeared quickly, swimming away to their new lives. He knew that turtles always came back to the very same beach they were born in to lay their own eggs. So someday when Razi was an adult he could be back here and see the babies of one of these same turtles.

It was a lovely feeling. But it couldn't completely dislodge the sadness that dimmed Razi's world, no matter how much the sun shone and waves danced.

The sun rose higher and prickled his skin. Then he saw something bobbing in the water. Something dark.

Razi squinted into the horizon. The turtles were all gone, but this was too big to be one of them anyway.

Whatever it was, it was heading toward land.

The sea glittered a brilliant, sparkling blue now, and the dark object swirled closer and closer to the shore with every wave.

It was a boat.

Razi stood up. This wasn't a fishing boat like the ones on Serendib. This boat was plain and simple, with no sail or outrigger, and, as it moved closer, Razi saw it had some strange lettering etched on the side.

*Foreign letters*, thought Razi excitedly. Where had the boat come from?

It dipped into a wave and then lifted up, a solitary blot on the empty ocean. As it surged closer, Razi saw something droop out over the side. Something small and bunched.

A hand.

An actual human hand! Someone was in the boat!

Razi staggered back, jabbing his foot on a pointed shell. The pain hardly registered as he watched the boat bobbing closer. He looked around the beach wildly to see if there was anyone to help. But, as usual, it was entirely deserted.

The boat swirled closer and Razi froze. Was he going to have to get into the water? Dread clawed his heart at the prospect.

A gull squawked overhead, startling Razi. It was the jolt he needed, and he ran into the sun-warmed water, soaking his clothes as he waded quickly toward the boat.

*This is okay, you can do this*, he told himself over and over as he tried to ignore the water rising to his chest.

Razi reached the boat and looked over the side. An egret swooped by and darted off again, leaving the echo of its cry.

Razi gulped.

Lying in the bottom of the boat, sunburned and still, was a boy.

# Chapter Three

"Okay now," said Razi. "Stay calm, *stay calm*, this is serious. Just BE CALM."

With all his strength he pulled the boat out of the sea and dragged it up the beach, making a groove in the soft sand.

The boy was on his side, cheek pressed against the bottom of the boat. His eyes were closed and his expression was blank. His lips were parched, and his skin was covered in patches of white where salt had dried. Even his clothes were dried up, and they rustled like paper when Razi shook his shoulder.

His eyes remained shut.

"Um, hello," said Razi. "Er, listen, are you alive?"

The boy was as still as a stick. The sun beat down on him mercilessly, frying his already parched body. He had to be moved to the shade and given some water immediately.

Razi took a deep breath and carried on talking to the boy, despite feeling foolish. "So I'm going to move you over there. Get you out of the sun." He leaned into the boat and grasped the boy under his arms.

To his surprise the boy slid out easily, as if he was no weight at all. Razi dragged him all the way up the sand to the shade of the coconut trees and laid him down. Out of the sun's glare, it was instantly cooler, and there was a soft breeze too.

The boy twitched, his eyes fluttered open slightly, and then closed again.

Razi almost cried with relief.

"Now, *that* is good," said Razi, trying to sound encouraging. It had worked for the turtle, after all. "You stay here—I'm going to look for some water."

He stood up and looked around.

Something out at sea caught his eye. Another boat, identical to the one the boy had been in. There were two men in the boat, and the taller of the two was standing up, gesticulating furiously at the beach while the other rowed to shore. Razi couldn't understand any of this. What was going on?

Razi emerged from the trees and walked down the beach to meet the men. The tall one, who was strongly built with close-cropped hair, immediately jumped into the water and ran to him. To Razi's alarm, he gripped him by the collar and lifted him off his feet.

Razi tried to scream. He blanched at the man's furious expression.

"Marco!" said the other man, coming up the beach. "That's not him."

The tall man shoved Razi away. He seemed angry that he'd got the wrong person. Razi turned to run, terrified. He had to get away from these men fast.

"Where is he?" yelled the one called Marco. He rounded on Razi. "You! You must have seen him."

Razi shook his head hard. Was the man talking about the boy on the boat? He wanted to say something, anything, but couldn't find the words.

"He must be around here somewhere," said the other man. "That's his boat over there. We'll find him."

"Find him and kill him," said Marco, kicking at a scuttling crab.

Razi began to tremble. The boy was lying unconscious just yards away from them in the shade of the coconut trees. He was weak and barely alive, and these men wanted to harm him. He couldn't let them do that.

"Oh! D-do you mean the boy in the boat?" said Razi, finding his tongue at last.

Marco stopped and turned around. "What do you know?"

"N-nothing," said Razi, which was true. He pointed toward Galle town, then carried on less truthfully. "He asked me where the closest town was, and I told him it's a mile up the beach. So he ran that way."

Marco came toward Razi slowly. His thick neck and meaty shoulders made Razi shrink away until he backed onto the side of their boat.

"When was this?" said Marco, breathing into Razi's face.

"An hour ago."

"Why did you say before that you hadn't seen him?" The man spoke slowly, making the words sound doubly dangerous.

Razi swallowed as he tried to think of a reason. "I wasn't sure what you m-meant. I m-mean, 'Where is he?'

doesn't mean much, d-does it? Now, if you'd said, 'w-where's that boy who came on the boat...'" He was blabbering and Marco was looking at him with deep suspicion. He should shut up before he brought some serious damage down on himself.

"I see." Marco still spoke slowly and deliberately. "If I find out that you've been lying to me, I will find you and I will kill you. Understand?"

"O-of course," stammered Razi. "That-that sounds clear enough." He caught himself before he blathered on anymore.

With that, Marco and his accomplice got back in the boat and rowed off.

# Chapter Four

Razi watched the boat heading in the direction of Galle.

He exhaled and pressed his hands to his forehead. What had he gotten himself into? He looked back toward the unconscious boy, his foot clearly visible for anyone to see.

He had to check that the boy was all right and then get out of there as fast as he could.

Razi ran to collect some fallen King coconuts. Once he'd found a pointed stone, he managed to pierce one, making a terrible mess, and felt the welcome squirt of cool coconut water on his face.

He went back to the boy and lifted his head up, tipping the King coconut slowly against his mouth. Half of the water sloshed out but the boy stirred awake and soon began to lap it up. He took in a good amount and then lay back down, his eyes closing again. He smelled of salt and the brininess of the deep sea. Razi felt a chill in spite of the heat of the day.

"Er, looks like you're a bit better then," said Razi, edging off and sitting back on his heels.

The boy opened his eyes. His face furrowed slightly and his eyes traveled all around him—taking in the jewel-bright sea, the shell-strewn beach with the boat pulled up high on the sand, and the bunches of bright orange King coconuts in the tree above him.

He blinked in confusion and tried to sit up. "Huh?"

"I said it looks like you're feeling better," said Razi, even though the boy probably couldn't understand him. He was clearly from a faraway land. "You're safe."

The boy looked at Razi for the first time. "Where is this?" he said, speaking Razi's tongue easily.

"Serendib," said Razi. "You're on the island of Serendib."

The boy lay back wearily but there was a hint of a smile on his face. He touched his chest and his clothes rustled again.

Razi stared at the boy. The rustling sound wasn't coming from his clothes after all. There was something long and cylindrical hidden inside his shirt.

The boy slowly began to lift himself up until he was leaning against the tree.

"Here," said Razi, prying the coconut open into two halves. He showed the boy how to scoop out the soft, pulpy insides. The boy took the coconut and scarfed it down gratefully. Seeing he was still hungry, Razi pierced open another King coconut for him, all the while keeping an eye out for the two men.

"What's your name?" asked the boy, after taking a long swig of coconut water. "I'm Zheng."

"I'm Razi. I live in the town down the beach from here. How come you speak our language?" He glanced nervously at the sea. Would the men be back? And was it all right to leave the boy in this state?

Zheng wiped his mouth with the back of his hand. "Oh, I speak *loads* of languages. I don't mean to boast, but I can't think of a language I don't know even a *little* of. Been all over the world, you see."

Razi frowned. So much for not boasting.

Zheng put down the coconut and gave a small sigh.

"Listen," said Razi. "I don't like to hurry you while you're like this, but you need to get out of here fast."

"Why do you say that?"

"Because a man called Marco means to kill you."

The boy startled and dropped the coconut, water sloshing over his legs. He scrabbled around as he tried to get up.

"Hold on!" said Razi. "I didn't mean that fast!"

Zheng stared at him with such panic-stricken eyes that Razi felt instantly sorry for him. "Who *are* you?" said Zheng. "Are you working for Marco?"

"No! He and another man came ashore in a boat soon after you did."

"Marco is *here*?" Zheng got up and staggered around like a crab before he managed to straighten up.

"Wait, where are you going?" said Razi, following Zheng as he stalked around in a panic.

"I don't know. Just *away*. I'll figure something out. I always do."

Razi could hardly leave him now. Zheng was shuffling inland in his ragged clothes, tired and weak, barely able to stand.

"Wait, Zheng." Razi ran up to him. "There's a place near here where you can rest for a bit."

Zheng turned back and looked at him hopefully.

"Come on!" Razi led the way up the beach, threading through the coconut trees to the abandoned fisherman's hut he knew was there. "It can't really be seen from the beach. You'll be safe while you hide and think of what to do."

The hut was just a minute up the beach, small and coconut-thatched. There was a single wooden window that didn't close very well. The corners were full of cobwebs, and the door hung lopsidedly off its hinges. It wasn't great, but it was safe.

"Would anyone come here?" said Zheng.

"No. It was abandoned a long time ago. No one comes to this beach at all. I only come here because of the turtles."

Zheng relaxed visibly and settled on the hard earth floor, stretching himself out.

"What's that rustling noise coming from your shirt?" asked Razi.

Zheng paled under his sunburn. "I'm not sure what you mean. I think it's my bones creaking."

Razi suppressed a chuckle. Whatever it was, clearly Zheng didn't want Razi to know.

"Thank you for everything," said Zheng. "The less you know about any of this the better. Marco is a dangerous man, and Cook isn't too sweet either."

"Don't I know it." Razi leaned against the window. "He's already threatened to find me and kill me if I was lying to him. And I was."

Zheng shook his head in confusion. "What are you talking about?"

"Marco asked if I'd seen you. I said you went to town and sent him the wrong way."

Zheng's face turned sour. "Oh no. He's not someone you want to cross for any reason."

"What about you, though? Will you be all right?"

"Of course," said Zheng, leaning his head against the wall and closing his eyes. He seemed to have become more relaxed after reaching the hut. "I've been in all sorts of situations. When you work on a ship and have been all over the world, you're ready for *anything*. Reminds me of the time we had to fight off pirates. Not that it happened just the once, but this one time was particularly tense, because I had only one working arm at the time."

Razi had no idea how seriously to take any of this. He was curious about Zheng, though, and felt responsible for him after rescuing him from the boat. "Who are you? How did you come to be in that boat?"

Zheng's face screwed up, as if he was trying to hold back some emotion. "I was on a merchant ship that sank."

"You're a ship's boy, then?"

Zheng nodded. "It might not sound like much. But I was very close to the captain, no less. And I've been *all* over the world. Been doing this since I was eight, and now I'm twelve. Imagine that."

That was impressive, but Razi wasn't about to admit it. He was twelve too, but he had never even left the area he lived in.

"Where did you say you were from again?" said Zheng.

"Galle," said Razi. "It's a town about a mile or so up the beach from here. There's nothing else around. If you go up the beach the other way there's a village, but that's even farther away than Galle."

"What were you doing here then?"

"I was watching turtle hatchlings. There are always loads of them here. I like to see them go safely to the sea. Did you know that's why they run to the sea so soon after birth? It's so they're safe from predators."

"That's nice," said Zheng, though he didn't look too interested in the turtles. Which wasn't surprising considering he was running away from a maniac who was trying to kill him.

"I've got to go now. My mother will be waiting for me. We usually have breakfast together before she goes to work. Good luck, Zheng."

"Ah, breakfast… Can't remember the last time I had it," said Zheng, a mournful expression on his face. "Well, goodbye, Razi. Thank you for everything."

Razi nodded and turned to go. He stopped at the doorway. He couldn't very well leave Zheng without food. The coconut pulp was hardly anything.

He turned back to Zheng. "Don't move from here. I'll bring you some food and water and then you can be on your way."

Zheng looked thrilled. "Could you hide my boat as well? If Marco comes back, it'll show him where I am. I'd do it myself if I wasn't so weak."

"Sure." Razi smiled. He'd move the boat, bring the food, and that would be the end of that.

# Chapter
# Five

Razi ran all the way home. When he got close to town he slowed down and approached cautiously, looking to see if Marco and Cook were there. He knew he was late for breakfast. His mother would be furious under normal circumstances, but ever since the accident she'd been far more lenient with him. She might have even left for work at the lace mill by now.

Razi's family lived in one of a line of fishermen's houses facing the beach.

Beyond was Galle town, with its narrow, cobbled streets and orange-roofed villas packed close together.

There was no sign of Marco or Cook, so he ran into the house and burst through the kitchen. Mother was cooking roti at the stove and the smell of warm coconut was in the air. His sister, Shifa, was sitting cross-legged on the mat with a plate on her lap. She was eating quite fast and barely glanced at him. She spent all her nonschool days at the medicine man's, learning how to make foul-smelling medicines and treating injuries and illnesses. Razi couldn't understand it himself, but Shifa was always in a hurry to go there.

Mother looked up and smiled at Razi. "Where have you been?"

"I went to see the turtles again. There were loads of them today." He put two roti on his plate and piled up a generous dollop of onion sambal from the clay pot.

"I have to leave soon," said Mother. "You two clear up here."

Razi picked up a banana leaf from the pile that was always on the side—cleaned and cut into squares for wrapping lunches.

He sat down and quickly wrapped one of the roti and some sambal in the banana leaf. He stuffed it in his pocket when he thought no one was looking.

"What are you doing?" said Shifa, pausing midbite.

Mother looked up from turning a roti.

"Eating," said Razi, nudging Shifa and looking at her meaningfully.

Shifa frowned in disapproval. She always went big sister on him, even though she was younger. Only by eleven minutes, but still. He'd explain to her later.

"I was just thinking, Razi." Mother had finished cooking and came and sat with them after serving herself some food too. "Nathan is going out of town for two weeks. He said you can use his boat, since it'll just be sitting there all that time. Maybe you could join the men when they go fishing tonight?"

Something like dread crept over Razi like a new skin. Not this again. "No, Mother, please. I can't do it."

Mother smiled sadly. "But you love fishing, Razi. You can't be afraid forever."

Razi shook his head hard. He just couldn't.

For once Shifa kept quiet.

Mother picked at her roti. Razi noticed her hands for the first time in ages. Her fingertips were raw and pink. It must be from the weaving loom; she'd increased her working hours lately to make ends meet. He stared at her hands guiltily. He should be helping more—then maybe she wouldn't always look so tired.

Mother went off to her work at the lace makers' yard and Razi quickly started the washing-up. As he scrubbed the blackened cooking pot, he hurriedly told Shifa about Zheng over the sound of the sloshing water.

Shifa stopped sweeping the floor to listen. "How on earth did you manage to get into such a mess before you'd even had breakfast?"

"*I* didn't do anything!" said Razi, scrubbing furiously. "I had to help Zheng, didn't I?"

"Yes, but you didn't have to make an enemy of those men. Why did you first tell him you didn't see the boy and then say you did? He must have been suspicious immediately."

"Well, I'm sorry I couldn't keep my cool when faced with a potential murderer. Now that I have some experience, I'll do better next time."

Shifa laughed. "Wait, so this boy's waiting for you to bring him food? He might need some medical help too. Go on, I'll finish up and meet you there."

"Great, thanks! Come as soon as you can." Razi took a change of clothes for Zheng and headed to the door.

"Be careful, Razi!" Shifa shouted after him. "Those men might try to follow you if they think you're hiding something."

Razi paused near the door and looked out, scanning the area for Marco and Cook. Some men were stilt-fishing, their crane-like figures dotted among the rolling waves. The sight of one of the stilts, empty for months now, made Razi's heart hurt. He slipped out with his head down and started the walk to the hut.

The sun was getting hotter now. Waves crashed on the shore, and the boat was still plainly visible on the beach. He slapped his forehead when he realized he'd forgotten to move it like Zheng asked him to. He'd do it just as soon as he put down the things he was carrying in the hut.

He entered and peered around as his eyes adjusted to the light. The hut was dark after the glare outside, and Zheng breathed noisily as he lay fast asleep on the floor. Razi pulled the door to behind him, leaving it ajar as it wouldn't close fully. Placing the clothes on the floor, he put the food parcel on the windowsill.

Just as he was about to slip out again, Zheng grunted and shifted in his sleep. He turned over, and something slipped out of his shirt and lay slightly wedged under him. Razi tiptoed up to him and leaned over to see what it was. It was a thin brown leather case with stitching in darker brown. A row of bronze-colored studs secured it closed.

Razi was overcome with curiosity. What on earth was so important that Zheng had left with that one thing from a sinking ship? And whatever it was, maybe it was the reason Marco was prepared to kill Zheng and anyone who helped him.

He really should leave it alone.

But then Zheng would be on his way and Razi would never know what all the fuss was about. A little look couldn't hurt.

Razi held on to the windowsill for balance and leaned over on one leg as far as he could. He reached out a hand and gently inched the case out from under Zheng. He hardly dared to breathe as he slid it free. The first bit came out easily, but then one of the studs snagged on Zheng.

Zheng snorted in his sleep and turned over again so he was now facing Razi. The leather roll was left behind him on the floor and Razi quickly snatched it up.

With trembling fingers he undid the studs, the faint pops sounding loud in the silence. The smell of ink drifted from inside as he opened the case to see what it contained.

# Chapter Six

As the case rolled open, Razi saw there was a scroll in the middle. It was sand-colored, thick, and heavy.

Suddenly the room brightened dazzlingly as the door scraped open.

Zheng opened his eyes and screamed to find Razi crouching over him. At the same time, Razi jumped out of his skin and sprang up screaming. The scroll fell off his lap. They both screamed at the dark apparition standing in the sunlit doorway. The figure then began to scream at their screaming.

"Stop it!" yelled Shifa, closing the door slightly. "Why are we all screaming?"

Zheng snatched the scroll and the open leather case from the ground with a shout. "You were trying to rob me!"

"No, I wasn't!" said Razi.

"Yes, you were!" Zheng pointed the scroll at Razi and then at Shifa. "And who's this? You've brought someone to help you rob me blind."

"What's there to rob?" said Shifa, looking confused. "We came to help."

"Oh, really?" said Zheng, putting the scroll back into the case and snapping the studs. He shoved it back inside his shirt. "With what?"

"I brought you this," said Razi, taking up the parcel of food from the windowsill. "And that's my sister, Shifa."

"I told you not to tell anyone," said Zheng. He took the parcel from Razi, though, and fell upon it with glee. He tore off a strip of roti and stuffed it into his mouth. "Thank you so much!"

He ate without stopping, mopping up the last of the sambal from the banana leaf with the roti.

He paused with his cheeks stuffed like pillows and pointed to Shifa. "You shouldn't have brought her, though."

"Don't worry, you can trust her. I tell her everything."

Zheng's face contorted comically as he swallowed quickly. "Did you tell anyone else?"

"No, just Shifa."

"Here," she said, "I brought you this." For the first time Razi noticed that Shifa was carrying a plant with long thick leaves that were prickly at the edges. He'd seen it growing all over town, and it looked like she'd just pulled it out of the ground; its roots trailed the bottom of her dress and clumps of earth had fallen at her feet.

Zheng looked bewildered as he took it. "Do I eat it?"

"No! It's for your skin. It's very burnt. Stay out of the sun until it heals, and if it stings anywhere just use this." She took out the knife she always carried around for collecting samples and slashed at one of the leaves, pointing to the slime oozing out of it.

Zheng looked revolted. He put the plant on the floor beside him and rolled up his empty food parcel. "I can't stay out of the sun. I need to get going now that I've eaten and rested."

"I'm not sure that's a good idea," said Shifa.

"I've got no choice."

"Where do you need to go?" said Razi.

"I don't have a clear idea but I will find my destination somehow," said Zheng grandly. "Tell me something. Do either of you know the sea around here well?"

"Razi does," said Shifa. "He's a fisherboy."

"A fisherboy?" Zheng looked stunned, then began to laugh. He threw up his hands and looked to the roof of the hut as if he couldn't believe his good fortune. "A *fisherboy*! Razi, you're *exactly* the person I need."

"I have no idea what you're talking about," said Razi. "And anyway, I don't fish."

"A fisherboy who doesn't fish?" said Zheng. "How interesting."

"It's complicated," said Shifa. "What do you want with Razi?"

"Well..." Zheng turned to Razi. "Do you happen to know if there's a rock in the middle of the ocean somewhere around here that is shaped like an elephant?"

Shifa looked at Zheng as if he was crazy.

But Razi knew exactly what Zheng was talking about. He knew the sea like the back of his hand. Elephant Rock was not on the routes that the fishing boats took, but he knew it all right. He'd been around there once with Father a long time ago, and he'd noticed the shape at once.

"I know it," said Razi.

"I knew I could count on you!" Zheng's face bloomed with happiness. "I need to get there at once."

"Why?" said Razi. "It's just a rock in the middle of the sea."

"It's on the way to somewhere I need to get to."

"Are you in some sort of trouble?" said Shifa.

"I haven't done anything wrong," said Zheng, "if that's what you're asking."

"Is this something to do with that scroll?" said Razi.

"Could be."

"Listen, there's not much we can help you with after this," said Shifa. "Razi's already in trouble because he lied for you. We're just concerned for you."

"Ha! Don't be," said Zheng. "The adventures *I've* had! The captain always said that I've had a more exciting life than *him* even. You're talking to someone who's survived a three-day sandstorm in a desert, getting flooded during the monsoons in a rain forest, and now being lost for a month at sea."

"A month?" said Shifa. "No one can survive a month without food or water."

"Hmm, maybe it was a week then," said Zheng.

"You just said a month!" said Shifa.

"A week, a month," said Zheng, swaying his hand to and fro. "Something like that."

"I'm sure," said Shifa, sighing. "So you need to go to this elephant rock?"

"Yes, it's very important that I get there quickly. I have a tiny request. Razi, could you take me?"

"What? No!" said Razi.

"Come *on*. You're local and you know the sea around here. You're the ideal person. Please say yes. I guarantee it'll be the greatest adventure of your life!"

"Why would you assume that going with you would be the greatest adventure of his life?" said Shifa.

Zheng looked out through the gap in the door to the deserted beach outside. "Not to be rude, but I don't see anything much happening here."

Shifa raised her eyebrows, but Razi could see his point. Zheng was a windstorm of excitement even if Shifa couldn't see it herself.

But the idea of going to sea was out of the question.

"I can't, sorry," said Razi. "I can explain how to get to Elephant Rock if you want."

"Razi, can I see you outside for a moment?" said Shifa.

Zheng opened the bottle of water Razi had brought and took a gulp. Razi followed Shifa outside. They stayed in the shelter of the trees.

"I don't think you should be telling him how to get anywhere," said Shifa.

"Why? I can't see what harm it'll do."

"We don't know anything about him. All those big stories—who knows if any of it's true? You're too trusting."

"But even if he's lying about the stories, there's nothing wrong with telling him how to get to Elephant Rock! You're too *un*trusting."

"Haven't you thought about why he might want to go there? Maybe he's in some kind of trouble. Maybe he's running away from the law."

Razi scratched his ear. He hadn't thought about that.

"I think you've done enough for him now," said Shifa. "We might be doing the wrong thing if you help him anymore."

"But if I help send him on his way, those two men will follow and then they'll be off my back! Haven't you thought of that?"

Shifa twisted the ends of her hair. "But what if Zheng is bad and the men are the good people?"

Razi was perplexed. "You're saying the good people are the ones wanting to kill Zheng, a child?"

Shifa opened her mouth, then closed it again. She couldn't argue with that so they went back into the hut.

Zheng was where they left him, leaning back against the wall. "Have you decided?"

"I'm happy to give you all the help I can without actually coming with you," said Razi, settling down on the ground for a conversation. "But on one condition: you tell us everything. We need to know the truth, Zheng."

# Chapter Seven

Zheng considered for a little while, his face changing from one expression to another as if he was debating with himself. "So if I answer your questions, you'll tell me all you know?"

Razi nodded. "For starters, what's that scroll you're carrying?"

Zheng opened the case and took out the scroll. He spread the thick paper out on his lap and for the first time Razi could see it properly.

"Ooh," said Shifa, all agog, reaching out for it.

Zheng whipped it away as if he didn't want them to have too much of a look.

"Is it a map?" said Razi, leaning forward.

It was. It was beautifully drawn in blue ink, showing the sea and little pieces of land. The cutoff land mass at the top looked vaguely familiar. On the right side of the map was the sun, its rays slanting into the rest of the illustration.

Razi drank in all the details. It was exquisitely done, labeled in tiny letters in another language, and parts were shaded blue to show the ocean. "What's it for?"

"Just to show where something, er, is," said Zheng, hurriedly rolling the paper up.

"Wait a minute," said Shifa, stopping him by plonking a finger on it. She tapped on an X shown on a little island. "I know what this is!"

Zheng gulped and pulled it away from her.

Shifa laughed in amazement. "I can't believe it! It's a treasure map."

"A treasure map?" Razi stared at Zheng.

Zheng nodded. "You want the truth? All right, I'll tell you the truth."

Razi and Shifa drew closer around him. Even the wind outside fell away as Zheng started his story.

"I was eight years old when I started working on the seas. My uncle knew the captain and sent me to him."

Zheng popped and unpopped the studs on the map case. He sounded different. Honest. As if he wasn't trying to sound brave and exciting anymore. "I never had much of a home before. I lived with my uncle because I had no parents, but he had a big family and they wanted to get rid of me. After he'd handed me over to the captain I never saw any of them again."

Razi's eyes widened. "What, never?"

Zheng nodded. "I lived in accommodations close to the docks when we weren't on the seas. But we were on the sea a lot, and I *loved* it. I love everything about it—the places we go, the people I'm with, having a family. I've sailed all over the world and seen so much. The captain was more of a father to me than my uncle ever was. He took me under his wing and he was so good to me. He taught me to read and write, and I could look at all his books anytime I wanted to. We were a merchant ship carrying luxury goods across the world."

"What sort of goods?" said Shifa.

Zheng closed his eyes, speaking with a kind of reverence. "We had rolls of the finest silks, threaded in the shiniest of golds and purples and scarlets. Reams of the softest cottons. The brightest ceramics from the world's best potteries. Great pots of pepper and saffron and cinnamon. And the smells! If only you could know.

The fragrance of amber, sandalwood, frankincense, cedar. The fluffiest wool rugs, the sparkliest of emeralds, lapis lazuli, jade..."

He spoke as if in a dream, and Razi was entranced. It was a world away from his own life.

"Everything was the best that money could buy. One of the most valuable things we carried was an ancient dagger. It was very famous, very historically important. It had been stolen from a temple years ago and then changed hands over and over for big sums of money. We were carrying it across the world, with some other smaller items in the collection."

Zheng paused and rubbed his forehead. "We would never deliver the Dagger of Serendib anyway—"

"Wait a minute," said Shifa. "Dagger of Serendib?"

The name sounded slightly familiar to Razi.

"Yes, it had belonged to an old Serendib king or something." Zheng shrugged. "Couldn't see the appeal myself. It was all dull and old looking."

"Dull and old looking!" Shifa looked furious. "The Dagger of Serendib is a thousand-year-old historical artifact from our country that was stolen and taken away from its rightful home."

"Oh yes!" said Razi, remembering. "We learned about it in school and everything. And it was on your ship?"

Razi looked at Zheng with a newfound respect. He really did have something to boast about after all. Even Shifa looked completely shocked.

Zheng shrugged, but Razi could tell he was extremely pleased at how impressed they were. He took a deep breath, then paused to build suspense. "However," he began. "The item was fated never to reach its destination. At some point on the journey, it went…missing."

"How could something like that just go missing?" said Razi. "From a ship? Someone must have known what happened to it."

"Oh yes," said Zheng. "And that someone is me. The Dagger of Serendib was stolen by the captain."

# Chapter Eight

"*The captain stole it?*" said Razi. "Your captain? The one who was like a father to you?"

"He wasn't going to keep it, you understand. He meant to return it."

"To whom?" said Shifa.

"To Serendib. The captain's one of your countrymen."

A prickle of excitement ran up Razi's spine. Shifa, in spite of her skepticism, was staring, enraptured. Here was Zheng, a total stranger from another world, with a wildly fascinating story that was creeping closer and closer to home with every word.

"So what happened?" said Razi.

"Marco, our first mate, suspected the captain right away, and he confronted him about it. He'd been planning to steal the dagger for himself, you see—not to do the right thing, but to sell it when we landed and keep the money for himself. The captain realized this and knew that Marco would stop at nothing to find where he'd hidden the dagger, so when we were passing Serendib—it's on the shipping route that the trade ships take as we go from east to west—he rowed to an islet off the coast early one morning and buried the treasure in a carved wooden box for safekeeping."

Zheng traced the shape at the top of the map, and Razi realized with a start that it was the very south of the teardrop shape of their own island country.

"The captain knew the place well, as it was where he'd grown up. He only told one person what he'd done. Me. When he returned he drew this map and he told me about it in case anything happened to him. He was very excited when he got back to the ship. He'd been to the islet as a boy thirty years ago, and he said it's amazing how constant and unchanging some things were."

Zheng trembled slightly as he began the next part of his story. "What we didn't know was how much Marco wanted the dagger, and to what extent he'd go to get it. We didn't know he'd commit mass murder."

Shifa let out a gasp.

"He had to act quickly," continued Zheng. "Realizing that we were due to sail into a storm, Marco and the cook drugged the evening meal so the entire crew would be out of action. That way, he could steal the dagger and escape the ship, and no one would be any the wiser." Zheng gulped. "The storm would see to that."

Razi looked at Shifa. She was transfixed, her hand over her mouth in horror. Zheng took a deep breath and continued. "I was ill that day and couldn't keep anything down so I didn't have any of the evening meal. I was up most of the night being sick and heard the storm battering the ship. I went up to help the crew and it was clear immediately that something was wrong. I found Marco coming out of the captain's room with the map. It was too late to save the ship or anyone in it, so I jumped into the lifeboat Marco and Cook were about to leave in. And I abandoned my ship and the captain and my friends. I left everything I've ever loved to be destroyed by the sea."

A rough wind blew in from the sea and the door creaked, breaking into the silence that followed Zheng's story. The boy was bent over, as if lost in the ocean on that dark night with the rain pounding on the waves, and his captain and everyone he loved on the sinking ship.

"And that's how you came to be on the boat and landed here," said Razi.

Zheng nodded. "The boat was tossed around for hours by the storm. I couldn't see anything, even the ship. In a way I'm glad I was spared the sight of it breaking up, and the debris, and…" Zheng closed his eyes, as if he couldn't bear to even imagine it.

Shifa was thinking hard, trying to collect her thoughts. "Wouldn't it be better," she said, "to hand the map to the authorities? Rather than look for the dagger yourself with Marco on your back."

"I don't know if people would believe me, a ship's boy from nowhere. Besides, there might not be time—what if Marco thinks he can find the dagger without the map? I have to find it first—I will *never* let them get it. The captain was doing what he felt was important to him, and I'm going to complete his mission no matter what Marco does to stop me."

"So if you find the dagger," said Shifa, watching him closely, "you'll return it?"

"Yes," said Zheng simply. "That's what the captain would want me to do."

Shifa nodded, but Razi wasn't sure she was convinced.

"Now that you know everything," said Zheng, "please take me to the islet, Razi. It would help me so much. This is important to your own country. Don't you want to be a hero?"

Razi's head was spinning. "I can't. I'm sorry."

"Be brave!" said Zheng. "Just like those little hatchlings are. Only the other day the captain said to me, *Follow the turtle, Zheng. It leads you to good things.*"

"What does that even mean?" said Shifa scornfully. "That makes absolutely no sense."

Zheng considered it for a moment. "That's true, actually. I have no idea what he meant."

Shifa sighed and bit her lip.

"Sea turtles have a great sense of direction," said Razi. "That's how the females can return after twenty years to the beach where they were born. Maybe the captain meant for you to follow the people who will lead you on the right path?"

"That's deep," said Zheng. "You should come with me, Razi."

Razi was stricken with panic.

Zheng was about to say something when Shifa cut in. "He can't do it. Please stop asking him."

"Why not?"

Shifa shrugged. "I'm sorry. It's not my story to tell."

"It's all right," said Razi. "You can tell him."

Zheng looked expectantly at Shifa.

"You were right earlier," she said. "Razi is a fisherboy who doesn't fish. Razi doesn't just love the sea, he's obsessed with it. His whole life, fishing was all he wanted to do. He used to go on the fishing boats with Father every morning that he didn't have school, and stilt-fish every sunset. But eight months ago everything changed."

Razi dipped his head as he felt the tears coming.

"Our father died in a freak accident in the deep sea," said Shifa quietly. "Razi hasn't gone back into the water since."

The sound of the thrashing waves outside amplified in the silence. Razi looked down into his lap. He hated talking about what had happened and hearing about it. He hated how it made him feel. How hopeless and angry and...guilty. What Shifa hadn't told Zheng was that Razi was supposed to have gone with their father that day but had been messing around with his friends and been too late. If he'd been there, could he have done something to save Father?

Zheng nodded as if he understood. Razi felt a stab of anger before he realized what Zheng had lost too.

He felt he had to say something. "There's no rule that says I have to go back to fishing. I'm happy to stay on land." Even as he said that he knew it was a lie. He had never been sadder in his life, but he couldn't go into the sea anymore. Where before he saw beauty and excitement, now all he saw was ugliness and misery.

He could never forgive the sea for what it had done.

"I'm very sorry to hear that." Zheng hunched down. He looked beaten. "Can I borrow a boat then? I don't want to use the one I have because it'll make it easier for Marco to find me."

"We don't have a boat anymore," said Shifa. "Because Father's… Well, you know."

"Oh yes." Zheng's face fell.

"Wait," said Razi, looking up. "I know where I can get you one. Our father's friend Nathan is out of town and Mother wanted me to go out in his boat sometime. She's been trying to get me to go with the other fishermen for ages. You could borrow that, then leave it here afterward."

Zheng's face brightened up at once. "When can I have it?"

"It'll have to be first thing tomorrow morning," said Razi. "When the catch has come in and everyone's distracted. I'll be able to get it then and bring it to you."

"Thank you!" Zheng beamed. "I'll take the boat, and then I'll be on my way!"

# Chapter Nine

The beach was always a carnival of sound early in the morning when the catch came in. Razi strolled through the bustle wearing a ragged straw hat pulled low over his head to hide his distinctive curly hair. Fishing boats were pulled high up on the beach, their rectangular sails flapping in the wind and great mounds of silvery fish spread out all over the sand. Hawkers yelled and buyers bargained, standing over glassy-eyed seer, mackerel, and bass. The breeze was salty with the smell of fresh fish. The traders came first, buying up big batches that they took away in carts, and then servants from the houses in town arrived, carrying away thickly sliced chunks of fish in brass basins to cook for lunch.

Razi wandered in and out of the crowds, dodging flying scales as fishermen expertly sliced and gutted fish with their sharp, curving knives. He was trying not to draw attention to himself as he made his way to where Nathan's boat was tied up, but then he saw something that stopped him in his tracks. Razi felt the familiar sadness that he carried everywhere being replaced by a cold, rising anger.

Father's spot on the beach had been empty since he'd died, but not today. Today, someone else was in it, haggling with a buyer over a mound of fat prawns. Next to it was a basket of particularly big seer fish with their tails trailing out on the sand. It was one of the newer fishermen in town, Nalaka.

His father's friend Sidath, who was selling fish nearby, called, "Come here, boy," to Razi, as if to spare him the sight.

"One minute," said Razi. He felt like a fiery spear had pierced right through his heart. How dare this man move into *their* spot? It was Father's and his. It was theirs forever. He walked up to Nalaka and stood staring at him until he stopped bargaining with the person he was with and turned to Razi.

"Yes? What do you want?" said the man impatiently.

Razi spoke with a quiet fury. "This spot is taken. You know that. Everyone here knows that."

A hush fell over the previously noisy beach. The buyer threw up his hands impatiently.

"This is a public beach," said Nalaka. "Anyone can stay anywhere. There's nothing to mark any *spot*."

Razi felt the heat sear into his heart even more. Father had always said they should never argue with another fisherman, not least because of the very sharp knives that both parties were usually carrying.

Sidath called over to Nalaka. "Hey, man, that's Raif's son. Leave him alone."

Nalaka shrugged. "Go away, boy."

Razi didn't budge. "Will you be gone by tomorrow?"

Nalaka sighed. "No, I won't be *gone by tomorrow*! Go away now."

"This is my father's spot!" yelled Razi.

"Run along before I give you a thrashing!"

"I will not run along. You need to tell me you won't be back here again."

"This is nonsense," said Nalaka, looking irritated. "Accept it, boy, and stop being a baby. Your father's not coming back. He's *dead*."

At that, whatever it was that had been keeping Razi's emotions in check tore apart. He snatched up a large seer by the tail and slammed it hard across Nalaka's face. The fish hit the man on the cheek with a resounding smack, leaving an imprint of redness and fish scales behind.

A collective gasp rippled through the crowd.

Nalaka froze, and the crowd fell silent. Sidath put his hands on his head.

Nalaka roared in humiliation and made a grab for Razi. Sidath quickly stepped in between them, pushing Razi away. "Get out of here, Razi!" he yelled.

Razi tossed the mangled fish aside and ran off like the wind, his heart pounding, his whole body shaking with rage. He shoved past two men in the way. *How dare he?* How could Nalaka speak about Father like that?

Razi thudded away down the beach, thrashing angrily through the wet sand and the waves. Without even knowing where he was going he found himself running toward *his* beach, toward Zheng's hut. He left the fishermen far behind, hurtling past the reef, past the boat, and into the trees, bursting into the hut where Zheng was stirring.

"I'll do it!" he yelled.

Zheng stared at him in confusion. He rubbed his eyes and squinted at Razi.

"I said I'll do it!" Razi fell onto his knees. "I can take you on the seas. I can sail you to the farthest corner you want. I know this sea like the back of my hand, and I can take you where you need to go. And we will bring back the dagger and I will be the son my father would want me to be!"

Zheng sat up cross-legged. "You mean it?"

"Yes, I do." Razi swallowed. "I think it's time."

"It's going to be dangerous," said Zheng. "Won't lie about that."

"I know!" Razi laughed. "And I'm not afraid."

He felt reckless. Alive. Ready to take on the world.

Zheng leaped up and embraced him. "Then let's do it!"

# Chapter Ten

Footsteps sounded outside and Shifa came into view. She was carrying some- thing as she hurried toward them, her hair whipping around her face.

"Razi, you idiot!" she said as she came in. "I heard about everything."

"What have you done?" asked Zheng, staring at Razi.

"I slapped a man at the market with a fish."

"You *slapped* someone with a *fish*?" Zheng howled. "Nice."

Shifa glared at Zheng as she dumped the things in her arms on the ground, then handed a parcel to him. "Here, some food for you. As for you, Razi, can we speak outside?"

Reluctantly, Razi left the hut.

"Razi." Shifa faced him, looking serious. "You must go and apologize to Nalaka."

"Me?" Razi was staggered. "Why me? He was the one who said all that stuff."

"*I* miss Father too, Razi." Shifa's eyes were moist. "I wish it had never happened. I wish we still had him. But you can't go around slapping people for staying in his spot. Nalaka's right. There is no spot. It's a beach."

Razi sighed and turned away from his sister. How could he explain it to her? That it was more than just a spot. It was a reminder that he couldn't step up. He couldn't be the son that his father would have been proud of. He had given up, and now the livelihood that they had built up was gone too.

"He could have been more understanding," said Shifa gently. "But he didn't do anything wrong. You did."

His heart fell a bit. Slapping another fisherman wasn't something his father would have felt proud of either. "All right, I'll apologize."

"Good," said Shifa. "Come on, let's go back in."

Inside, Zheng was finishing up his meal. Empty mangosteen shells lay on the floor beside him. He was collecting into the banana leaves. He looked up apprehensively at Razi. "You're still all right to come with me, aren't you?"

"Yes, I am."

"What's this?" said Shifa.

"I'm taking Zheng on the boat to find the treasure."

"Oh no, Razi! This is because of Nalaka, isn't it?"

"Why is it a problem?" said Razi, his anger flaring up. "This is what you and Mother have been trying to make me do for ages!"

"We just want you to be the old Razi again. We want you to be happy. Not go following someone who"—she turned to Zheng for a second—"no offense, might not even be telling the whole truth."

"Hey! I *am* telling the truth," said Zheng.

"Are you calling him a liar?" said Razi.

"No! I just think he *may* be lying, which is a reasonable assumption when you don't know someone."

"Listen, I don't want to come between you two," said Zheng.

"You're not," said Razi. "I trust you. It's Shifa who doesn't."

"That's not true," she said. "I don't distrust you! I just don't necessarily *trust* you."

"This is crazy."

"No, what's crazy is you going off with someone you hardly know on a dangerous mission, when you haven't been able to face the sea in eight *months*."

"I'm doing it anyway."

"Fine!" Shifa went to the stuff on the floor that she'd brought with her and fished something out. "If you're going with him, I won't stop you. But I'm going to need to make a copy of that map."

# Chapter Eleven

"Why do you need a copy of the map?" said Razi.

Shifa sighed with impatience. "If you're going with him, I need to have an idea of where you'll be. What if you get into trouble?"

"So much bureaucracy," said Zheng. He tossed the leather case onto the floor.

Shifa got to work with a quill and ink. Razi crouched down on the packed-earth floor and peered around his sister as she set the map and a blank piece of paper side by side in front of her.

"Actually, you do it," she said, pushing the blank sheet to Razi. "Your drawing is so much better."

Razi sketched out the map quickly, inking in the land masses and the sea. He handed it back to her.

"No, wait, what about the labels?"

Razi considered the map and pointed with the quill. "So that's where we are now." He wrote down *Turtle Beach*.

"And this is the rock you were asking about?" Shifa said, pointing to something that didn't look much like an elephant at all.

Zheng nodded.

"Is that what the label says?" said Shifa. "*Elephant Rock*?"

Zheng nodded again, and Razi wrote down *Ananda Rock* there.

Shifa glared at him. "Ananda? The name of the Queen's elephant? Razi, take this seriously."

"I just don't feel the need, that's all! What does this say, Zheng?" he said, pointing at a part of the map close to the islet where the treasure was supposed to be buried. There was something like a cluster of broad snakelike creatures drawn there.

Razi thought he saw Zheng hesitate for a millisecond before he answered. Had he imagined it?

"Sea of Monsters," said Zheng.

"Seriously?" Shifa looked at Razi, then back at Zheng. "Seriously—Sea of *Monsters*?"

Zheng shrugged. "They might seem unbelievable to you, sea monsters. But having seen the things that *I've* seen, it's not surprising at all. You should open your mind a bit."

Shifa snorted. "I *do* have an open mind. I just don't believe in monsters, that's all."

"Zheng has a point, actually," said Razi. "We know very little about the ocean. So little of it has been explored by humans. They say that even centuries in the future we might have only explored a tiny fraction of it."

Shifa ignored that interesting tidbit and turned to Zheng. "So you want Razi to come with you to this, this...*Sea of Monsters*?"

"Oh, don't worry," said Zheng quickly. "They don't mean any harm. They're quite gentle really."

"Really?" she said. "A bunch of gentle sea monsters?"

"Yes, really," said Zheng. "Nothing to worry about. Did I tell you about the time a giant squid—"

"Zheng, you can talk the gills off a mackerel," said Shifa. "We don't need to hear this now. Just write it down, Razi."

Razi faithfully wrote down *Sea of Monsters* on their map. He glanced at Zheng and saw a guilty look flit across his face.

Was he making a mistake? Was Shifa right to be suspicious?

"So this is where the treasure is," said Razi, tapping the *X*. It showed a small islet seemingly in the middle of nowhere, but over on the southwest there was a whole heap of smaller islands. The treasure islet had no label on it.

"Do you think you can get us there?" said Zheng.

Razi considered the map and tried to picture it in his mind's eye. He'd never gone as far out to sea as the islet but he had a good feel for direction. Neither Father nor any of the fishermen had the type of fancy equipment Zheng's shipmates must have had, but they traveled these seas and knew them well. "I'm sure I can."

Shifa compared the minute details of the maps before rolling them up. "All done," she said, handing Zheng back his case.

At that moment two men burst into the hut. Razi barely had time to get over the shock before he registered who they were.

Marco and Cook!

They shoved past him to Zheng.

"There he is!" yelled Marco. Zheng quickly stuck the pouch down his shirt before the man pulled him by the scruff of his collar and shook him like a leaf. "Where is it?"

"I don't have it," said Zheng in a strangled voice.

"Hey!" said Razi. "What are you doing?"

"You! I'll deal with you in a minute, you little liar," growled Marco.

Shifa backed away out of the hut and picked up a stick lying on the ground.

Cook pushed Razi away. "You little rat," he bellowed. His eyes fell on Shifa brandishing the stick. "Marco, the girl has the map!"

He lunged toward her, knocking Razi down.

"Run away, Shifa!" shouted Zheng at the top of his voice. He'd escaped from Marco and was trying to stop Cook. "Go, Razi, before they kill you."

Razi hesitated. Then he ducked out and grabbed Shifa, pulling her away from the hut. Marco gave a yell and followed after them while Zheng struggled with the cook.

The twins ran toward town with Marco hot on their heels. When they were hidden from his view by some tall rocks on the beach, Shifa threw herself over a thick row of bushes growing to the side.

Razi followed and they rolled under the bushes.

"Ouch," he whispered. The leaves had little thorns at the ends and lilac berries of some sort.

Shifa looked at him. "I should have warned you— these are prickly pear bushes. We use the oil in some of our medicines. Be careful, the thorns are really sharp."

They heard Marco running closer and then stop. He seemed to be wondering where the children were.

Razi held his breath. Marco shuffled in place, centimeters from the bushes, unsure which way they'd gone. Razi knew they had the benefit of knowing the land, whereas Marco was a complete stranger.

Razi tensed as Marco's hand brushed against the bush above them. The man yowled and jumped away from the bush, shaking his hand in pain as blood ran from a nasty scratch.

"Interesting," whispered Shifa. She took out her knife and cut off a leaf from the bush above them. She dropped it into her pocket and hissed, "This could turn out useful—"

Razi shushed his sister. He was more interested in what Marco was doing. Peering carefully through the prickly leaves, Razi saw that he had stopped and was looking toward Galle. Over the man's shoulder, Razi could see the beachfront, with children flying kites, and the town houses with wide verandas beginning where the more modest fishermen's houses stopped. The smell of frying prawns came from the food cart selling freshly made fritters on the beach.

After a few moments, Marco gave up. He couldn't very well chase two children through a crowded town. He turned back slowly toward the fisherman's hut and Zheng, breathing raspingly.

Razi waited till he had gone a fair way before crawling out from under the bush. "Stay here," he said to Shifa.

He ran stealthily after Marco, keeping his distance. He saw the men try to stuff Zheng into a boat while he struggled furiously. Razi started toward them, then stopped. He wasn't a match for these men, and there was no point in both of them getting kidnapped. His hands were clammy as he watched.

Should he run back to town for help? Surely they'd let Zheng go when they found the map on him? Why would they need him when they had the map?

But they didn't let Zheng go, and Razi watched in terror as the boat cruised away into the distance.

He looked back to see Shifa approaching.

"They took him away!" he screamed. "Shifa, they took him away! What have I *done*?" The thought of the powerfully built Marco turning his anger on Zheng made him feel sick with horror.

Shifa was trembling. The full enormity of what had happened had only just hit them.

"Why would they do that?" Razi's heart was pounding. "They could have just taken the map and let him go."

Shifa twisted the ends of her hair around her shaking fingers. "W-what if they want revenge on Zheng?"

Razi's insides contracted with pain. "We have to help him. Those men are dangerous. They were prepared to murder the entire crew of a ship in the hope of getting rich. What would they do to Zheng?"

"I th-think for the moment Zheng is safe."

"How can you say that?"

"Because his map is only partly useful to the men," said Shifa. "Until they figure out what the labels mean and find the treasure, I don't think they'll do anything to him."

"What do you mean, figure out the labels?"

Shifa looked distraught as she slid something out of her pocket. A thick brown scroll, something too important looking to be the map Razi had drawn. She unrolled it and held it up. Her expression was wracked with guilt.

"I swapped the maps, Razi. We have the real one."

# Chapter Twelve

"What?" Razi gawked at the map, with its intricate details and markings on the thick paper. "How? I saw Zheng tuck it into his shirt."

"You saw him put the leather case in his shirt, but I swapped the maps so that he has your copy."

"Why did you do that?" asked Razi.

"Because I thought he wasn't telling us the truth!" said Shifa, crying. "And you were going to go off with him! I thought I'd take it to my teacher, Miss

Nabeeha. She knows everything there is to know about any topic, and if she doesn't, she knows how to find out. She could help translate the labels before you went off."

Razi remembered Zheng's hesitation when he was translating the map. "I would never think to do such a thing."

"This is exactly what I mean! You'd go on a mission across the seas with someone you don't know just on his say-so."

Razi was silent. Was she right?

"How would the copy of the map not be useful to them?" he said. "They can't read our words, but they could get them translated."

"Yes. *Turtle Beach, Ananda Rock, Sea of Monsters.* Doesn't say much, does it? Would they even recognize that it was the Galle coast?"

That was a good point. "Do you think they'll come back after us?" said Razi after a moment.

"I'm sure of it," said Shifa. "They don't look like the type to give up easily. Once they realize they can't get the details out of Zheng they'll come for us. They think we're all in this together!"

"We kind of are now," said Razi.

They sat in silence for a bit, the sea throwing spray on them.

"There's something else," said Razi. He'd been feeling terrible, but this admission made him feel even worse. "Do you know how the men found Zheng?"

Shifa cocked her head to one side and looked at him intently, her cheeks streaky with tears. "How?"

"It was me," said Razi. "I led them to Zheng."

"What are you talking about?" said Shifa. "You didn't lead them to Zheng."

"Not deliberately." Razi buried his head in his hands. Again and again in his head he saw Zheng being pulled into the boat and kidnapped. And the image of Zheng's own boat on the beach.

"How then?"

"I should have been keeping a low profile. Instead, I go and slap a man with a fish in the middle of a busy beach."

Shifa groaned.

"I've been so stupid and wrapped up in myself. Zheng has bigger problems than me, and I led them straight to him. What if Marco and Cook saw me making that scene and followed me to Zheng? And to make it worse I forgot to hide his boat. He *asked* me to do it and I had so many chances but I just kept forgetting."

Shifa was twisting her hair up in her fingers, cutting red lines into her skin. "It's not your fault; it's mine. I shouldn't have swapped the maps. I just wanted to check out Zheng's story, but I should have been more trusting, like you. If I had been, he'd have the proper map and they might have just let him go." She paused. "We need to help him, don't we? Because, because…"

Razi's chest contracted. He'd never been so frightened in his life. "Because, intentionally or not, *we* did this to him."

"He doesn't have anyone else to look out for him," said Shifa. "Everyone who cared about him died on that ship."

A mist was clearing in Razi's mind. He knew what they had to do. His heart thudded and his hands were slick with sweat, but he knew they had to do it. "Of course. We have to give Marco and Cook what they want in exchange for Zheng. We have to go and find the dagger ourselves."

# Chapter Thirteen

No one noticed Razi as he took Nathan's boat. A few of his former fisherboy friends were thrashing around in the sea, their laughter the only noise on the empty beach. They didn't see Razi as he started rowing. Their drifting apart had happened very slowly in the months after Father's death. Razi couldn't blame them really. He'd rejected the thing that had bonded them, and it had been hard to find common ground after that.

He sailed off apprehensively, keeping as close to the shore as he could. No one was in this stretch of sea. The beach had been fully cleared of the remains of fish by hungry birds, and everyone was either at home resting or going about their day in town.

This was the first time he'd been in a boat since the accident. Razi knew he had no choice but to do this, but his limbs were stiff and cold with trepidation. When he'd agreed to go with Zheng there was going to be another seafaring person with him. But now it was going to be just him and his sister. Shifa, for all her cleverness, was very much a landlubber and not much use at sea.

She was waiting for Razi near the hut when Nathan's fishing boat turned to the shore. She'd gathered their supplies in a round-bottomed cane basket, a green scroll nestling among a bag of mangosteens. It was the map, for which Shifa had quickly stitched a case. She'd also remembered to bring a spade.

"Good thinking!" said Razi, hauling in the things she passed him. He gave her a hand and she clambered into the boat.

"What's the point of that?" said Razi, nodding toward the scroll in the case Shifa had made. "Won't it get wet anyway?"

Shifa leaned out and dipped her fingers in the water. She splashed some on the scroll case. "It's made of lotus leaf," she said. "It repels water."

"Or we could put it in a bottle," said Razi, seeing the water bottle she'd collected from Zheng's hut.

"Let's do both, for extra protection." Shifa picked up the empty glass bottle and slipped the scroll in, replacing the cork tightly. She'd brought a gallon of water anyway, and had been bent diagonal with the weight as she'd lugged it over to the boat.

Razi pushed off. "What about Mother? You know with all she's been through we can't have her worrying that something bad has happened to us."

"We'll have to be back before nightfall so she won't even know. We find the treasure, grab it, save Zheng, and get home as soon as possible."

"That's quite a plan, but yes, we have to get back before she misses us."

"I hope—" Shifa broke off midsentence and screamed.

A hand fell on Razi and shook him roughly.

"Where is it?" said Marco, jumping into the boat, his lower half wet from wading in after them. Razi twisted from under him and pushed him away. The boat rocked and the man grabbed at Razi again. The sea pushed the boat out as he struggled against Marco's grasp. Out of the corner of his eye, Razi saw Shifa jab Marco sharply with the spade, pushing him against the side of the boat, which shook violently.

He roared and made a grab at her but she ducked away. Razi pushed him down again, sending him crashing into the food basket so that the mangosteens bumped out and rolled all over the boat. Marco's gaze fell on the bottle and he grabbed it.

"NO!" Razi lunged at him and knocked the bottle out of his hands. Shifa swooped to catch it but Marco snatched at it wildly. The bottle hit the side of the boat with a crash. It smashed into pieces and the map fell into the sea.

# Chapter Fourteen

The map in its lotus-leaf case bobbed away on the waves.

"NO!" yelled Razi again. Without the map they'd never be able to find the treasure or save Zheng.

Razi jumped into the open water, followed swiftly by Marco. The map swirled out of reach.

Razi struck out after the map, kicking the man out of his way. "Row away, Shifa!" he yelled to her.

Shifa was staring at him petrified, like a seer caught on a line. What was wrong with her? He planned to get the map and then swim after the boat. If she got far enough away, Razi was sure Marco would have to turn back. He didn't seem to be a very good swimmer. But first Razi had to get the map.

Finally Shifa seemed to get the message and rowed away on the boat. Razi reached the map first and seized it. He struck out toward the boat but Marco grabbed him by his foot and yanked him underwater.

Underneath the surface, the coral on the seabed glinted with myriad colors, bony fingers of bright oranges, yellows, and pinks speckled by shoals of darting red-striped fish. A turtle rose up from the bottom, paddling gently as rays of sunlight strobed through the water. The blood rushed loudly in Razi's ears as he struggled to breathe. He wedged the map in the coral and turned to fight off the man.

Marco let go immediately and dived to the map, which had come loose and was drifting up toward the surface.

Razi broke the surface and took in gulps of cool, fresh air. His chest ached with the effort of staying down too long. But in a few seconds he'd caught his breath and struck out behind the man again.

Marco had the map! He was swimming toward the shore. Razi sneaked up behind him and bit him hard on the shin. The man yelled and twisted around, cuffing Razi on the head. Razi darted forward and yanked the map from him. He turned over and used the man's head to kick off from, propelling himself forward toward the boat. Razi swam fast but Marco was hot on his heels again. Perhaps he was a better swimmer than Razi had thought.

He was tiring from the effort of fighting Marco off. The big man was within arm's length now but Razi couldn't go any faster. His exhaustion turned to horror as he felt the beginnings of a cramp. He was doomed. He couldn't do it anymore. He felt himself slow down in spite of his best efforts.

Then Razi was pulled clean out of the water and tossed down onto something hard. The wind was knocked out of him and he lay there, gasping, the map clutched tightly in his fingers. He blinked water out of his eyes.

He was back in the boat! He pulled himself up to peer over the side. Marco was in the water, left far behind them as Shifa powered the boat through the sea, her hair flying madly in the wind.

# Chapter Fifteen

Nathan's boat was very similar to Father's. It was pretty much the same as all the other fishing boats, except for the turtle he'd painted on the side. Shifa pulled its oars through the quiet waves. Marco was far behind now, wading to the shore in his wet clothes.

"Are you okay?" said Shifa.

Razi sat up and looked down at himself in dismay. "Yes, a bit wet, that's all."

"No, I meant in *other ways*."

"Huh?" Razi stared at his sister.

"Never mind."

"Oh." He was startled when the rupee dropped. "I...I'd actually forgotten."

It was strange. But all his focus was on how important the map was in saving Zheng's life. And when it came down to it, it was as if Razi had never been away at all.

Shifa smiled. "Good." She steered the boat farther on. "And I'm glad you're okay. For a minute there I thought he'd got you."

"I know," said Razi, thinking of his bursting lungs. "Just wondering why you didn't whack him hard on the head with the spade? You could have saved me a lot of trouble."

"Don't be silly," she said. "Hit him on the head? That could cause him permanent damage."

"He was trying to do *me* permanent damage."

"Still," she said. "I'm trying to be a healer, not a destroyer."

Razi huffed and unrolled the map. He had to admit, Shifa's idea for the pouch had been clever. The map wasn't completely dry, but it was only slightly damp. Nothing that a bit of sun wouldn't sort out.

"I know how to get to Elephant Rock easily," said Razi. "From there, I don't think it'll be that hard to find the islet. It's all by itself to the west of the rock. If we come to a cluster of five we know we've gone too far."

The land was way behind them now. Very soon they'd be in open seas, with nothing around them but the aquamarine water. The sea had deepened into a rolling, undulating green. Razi looked into its depths and his head spun. They were in very deep water, bluish green and almost clear. Pods of dolphins accompanied them now and then, arcing and sometimes spinning in the air, their splashes and the oars the only sounds in the stillness.

"The sea looks so beautiful, doesn't it?" said Shifa, glancing around at the endless blue. Waves crested and ebbed gently and all else was still.

Razi shrugged. He knew her words were for his benefit. She wasn't interested in the ocean at all.

"We should be coming to Elephant Rock soon, no?" It seemed like they'd been sailing for ages. Shifa shielded her eyes and looked at the horizon. "How long have we been traveling?"

"About an hour," said Razi. "Once we see the rock we'll head west through the Sea of Monsters. Come on, let's swap now."

Shifa scoffed as they changed places. "I hope you don't believe Zheng's nonsense about monsters. I wonder what that label actually said."

"There it is!" Razi pointed to the rock, which rose out of the water looking for all the world like an elephant raising its trunk to the sky. From one angle you could even make out tusks. Terns squawked and circled over its head. They'd built nests in all the nooks and crannies of the rock.

"Okay, we're on track! West now," said Shifa, the map spread out on her lap and her voice shivering with excitement.

Razi rowed under the arch of the rock, the birds getting louder and flapping into the air from their rocky perches as the boat went by.

They sailed on, leaving the rock far behind. The ocean was vast around them, and they were a tiny dot in it. Razi hoped Marco didn't catch up with them here. The wind blew west, bringing the faint cry of terns from the rock they'd left behind.

Shifa was twisting her hair around her fingers.

"What's the matter?" said Razi. He knew her sign of nervousness well.

She looked a bit unsure. "I-I'm sure it's nothing."

"But?"

"I thought…I thought I heard something."

"It's the birds," said Razi.

She nodded slowly. "Yes. Although this sounded a bit…different."

"In what way?"

"Like…a throb."

Razi giggled. "I don't hear it. But it doesn't sound that alarming."

Shifa smiled, but it didn't quite reach her eyes. She seemed on edge. Scared almost.

Razi kept on west. He couldn't do with Shifa losing her nerve. The day was getting hot and he wiped his brow.

Suddenly out of nowhere came a low, haunting moan. So low he wasn't sure if he'd heard it.

Razi stopped rowing. What in the name of everything fishy was that?

Shifa's hair was twisted around all her fingers now. She looked around the boat wildly, as if searching for something.

This was crazy. The wind had to be carrying the sound from land somewhere. There were no moans or groans on the high seas. This was different from a dolphin's whistle or click too. Razi decided to ignore it.

"We're well on target for the islet," he said, with what he hoped was a companionable casualness. The last thing he wanted was to spook Shifa. "We should be coming to the Sea of Mons—"

He stopped as a horrid realization hit him. Shifa wasn't looking at him. A low, deepwater sound reached his ears.

*Throb, throb, throb, throb. Throb, throb, throb, throb.*

Terror hit Razi like a ton of mullet slapped on the beach. The Sea of Monsters was real. Zheng hadn't made it up. There was such a place.

Shifa had gone pale.

Razi looked into the water.

The sea under them had gone gray and mottled. As he watched, the darkness spread out around them, getting bigger and bigger, as if something was rising from the bottom of the ocean.

# Chapter Sixteen

"Razi," said Shifa, speaking without moving her lips. "What. Is. That?"

Something was moving underneath them. Something huge...something bigger than a house and with gray, blotched skin.

He tried to keep the terror out of his voice. "It's—it's a shark. It's a shark. Look, it's a shark." His voice went very high at the last *shark*.

Shifa nodded, looking anything but convinced. "Of course. It's a shark."

*We are finished*, thought Razi.

The shadow underneath the boat glided out in front of them, the water hardly moving as Razi watched it move away. Just when he thought it was leaving them alone, the water splashed and it turned back toward them. A humongous head dipped up and came toward the surface.

Shifa's scream was muffled by her hands. A gigantic pointed face emerged; tiny eyes, turned-down mouth.

Razi leaned forward. Was that…?

A fountain of water gushed high into the air from its head as it boomed toward them. The unearthly cry twanged the air again, but this time Razi wasn't afraid.

"Shif, it's okay," said Razi, but Shifa stared, transfixed, at the creature by the side of their boat. It was as long as six town houses. It glided through the turquoise waters, its back topped by a ridged, glistening spine. As they watched, it blew another mountain of sea spray high into the air.

Razi leaned out for a better view, but Shifa was dumbstruck, beads of spray from the whale clinging to her face.

The whale groaned, that keening sound that Razi couldn't quite hear. As if it was there but not there at all.

Without warning, the whale jumped clean out of the water. Razi screamed involuntarily and Shifa rocked toward the other side of the boat.

It sailed over their heads and time slowed right down. Droplets of water sprinkled off the silvery head, catching the sunlight as they broke into thousands of tiny prisms. The pale underbelly followed, its ridged skin stretching and loosening as its gigantic muscles strained in movement. Clusters of barnacles pockmarked the enormous body soaring powerfully over them. Razi and Shifa shrank under the whale, their mouths stretched in silent screams as the mammoth shadow blotted out the sky.

It fell into the water with a crash on the other side. The boat rocked in place, waves splashing over the sides and drenching them both.

Razi exhaled in wonder.

He'd never seen anything more beautiful in his life. The whale swam away toward the horizon, where the line between sea and sky merged into the same deepening blue. Parts of its blue-gray back broke the surface now and then, revealing its course as it swam into the distance.

Shifa pressed her fists to her eyes. "What was *THAT*?" she exploded. She was shaking.

"They look scary but they're harmless," said Razi. "So *this* is Zheng's Sea of Monsters, isn't it? He was right all along."

"Argh, Zheng and his stupid—" Shifa seemed to make a conscious effort not to lose her temper. "What was that?"

"A blue whale! I didn't know we had them in these parts. Father said he saw one once, a long time ago, but he thought it had strayed from somewhere else. I can't believe it! How lucky are we."

"That *size*." Shifa shuddered. "And the sea around here is full of them?"

"Looks like it. But they really aren't dangerous, you know. And I think they're quite solitary, so we won't see loads of them together."

"Very comforting, but seeing that one was plenty, thank you very much."

Just as the words were out of her mouth, they saw two more blue whales swimming in the distance. Shifa let out a low moan as one of them doubled back toward them.

It came up close to them and bumped their boat gently. Water splashed against the side of the boat and Razi laughed.

"What is it doing?" Shifa had pressed herself to the side farthest away.

"It's just trying to be friendly. Look, it's the same one that jumped over us. It has some kind of scarring on its back."

She leaned over the boat to look at the several clefts on its back. "How did he get those?"

"Could have been a ship," said Razi. "Sometimes they cause serious injuries or even death. I think it's a she, by the way. Just guessing. The females are larger."

The whale came up and bumped the boat again.

"I wish she'd go away." Shifa's voice was very small and she looked frightened out of her mind. "She's so big and this boat is so small and we're in the middle of the ocean with nothing else around."

"She just wants to play." Razi smiled and called out to the whale. "Stop scaring my sister, Maalu."

"Maalu?"

"She needs a name, doesn't she?"

Maalu breached again, but thankfully a little away from the boat this time.

Razi laughed. "Now she's just showing off!"

Shifa didn't seem impressed. If anything she was even more nervous. Razi couldn't blame her. The sheer size of the animal was mind-boggling. Maalu came up and touched the boat with the tip of her nose and Shifa gripped the side, white-knuckled.

"Nothing's going to happen, Shifa. She's harmless."

But Shifa screwed up her eyes tightly as the boat rocked from Maalu's movements.

Razi got up and kneeled over the side. The whale was very persistent. He'd have to try to send her away before Shifa fainted with fright.

"What are you doing?" said Shifa, alarmed.

Before he could answer, Maalu jabbed at the boat and Razi fell into the sea.

# Chapter Seventeen

The shock was greater than the physical impact as Razi hit the waves. He sputtered as he sank into the depths, the water getting cooler as he plummeted downward. The blue-tinted world around him flapped in slow motion and a clump of seaweed floated past as he gazed at the sandy seabed far below.

Automatically, his body responded. His legs kicked out and pushed him up, his head breaking the surface to see Shifa looking worriedly over the boat. Water sloshed at his back as something big slid past. He turned to see Maalu frolicking in the water near him.

She dipped down into the depths, tail slapping the water. Without thinking, he dived after her.

Maalu glided through the water and spun around, circling Razi. His heart soared and he paddled toward her, marveling at her size and majesty. He wasn't afraid. She was magnificent. Her head flashed past again as she swam around him, so close he could put out his hand and touch her.

He kicked up to the surface, and she glided up too, both of them breaking the water at the same time. Razi gulped in a mouthful of air while Maalu sprayed a fountain of water through her blowhole.

"Look, Razi!" yelled Shifa. She was laughing and screaming and clapping her hands all at the same time. "Behind you!"

Razi turned around. Behind Maalu the sea was studded with more whales. A whole pod of them, this time a different species, with rectangular heads and small, cheeky eyes. Maybe thirty of them, swimming serenely in the great ocean without a care in the world.

For some reason he couldn't understand, Razi began to cry. He let himself slip down underwater to better watch them, becoming a tiny blot among these magnificent monsters of the ocean.

He came up to the surface again and Shifa gave him a hand as he clambered into the boat. From here, the view was even more glorious. The water was a clear sapphire around them, the pod of whales speckling it in hues of silver. Maalu swam away into the distance.

Razi sat down in the boat in his soaked clothes and began to sob properly. Shifa wordlessly passed him a gunnysack from the boat to use as a towel and took over the oars.

She patted his arm before they pulled away.

Razi shivered in his wet clothes as they cut through the water. He had never been more exhilarated in his life, but the tears came thick and fast at the same time. Shifa didn't say anything, but after a minute when his tears didn't abate she leaned over and hugged him tightly. He broke down completely and sobbed on her shoulder even more.

Zheng winced as his head thudded repeatedly against the side of the boat. He was on the floor, having been tossed there unceremoniously by Cook after he'd refused to tell them anything useful about the map.

Marco was sailing, and they zipped through the water at top speed. He'd hired a boat in town and this one was quite marvelous, as boats went. But Zheng wasn't too worried. He may be bound and gagged in a boat with his sworn enemies, but it was *nothing* compared to some of the other scrapes he'd been in.

"The boy was lying again," said Marco to Cook over the sound of the waves. His voice was angry, frustrated. "There's no temple in the middle of the sea where a blue-haired hermit lives."

Zheng snorted behind his gag. He'd persuaded Marco not to kill him by promising to explain the map. But he'd set him on the wrong track. After hours of searching, Marco had risked showing the map to a fisherman to decipher. Unfortunately, the man had set Marco right.

"The fisherman said it's a rock shaped like an elephant," continued Marco. "I'm sure the children must have passed there by now."

Zheng wasn't sure whether to be happy or disappointed that Razi and Shifa were on the trail of the dagger. It was great that they were doing this, but really, they didn't have the kind of expertise Zheng did.

"There it is!" said Cook.

Squawks filled the air. From Zheng's angle he could see the top of a high rock full of birds' nests as they navigated under it. He was annoyed to see that it was Elephant Rock. Never mind, he hoped Razi and Shifa were well out of the way by now and on the islet.

Cook turned back and gave a kick at Zheng. "We'll get you for this, you liar."

"Leave him for now," said Marco dismissively. "We'll punish him when it's time. He might yet prove useful."

Most people would cower at that, but not Zheng. The time he'd been thrown in a cage to fight an enraged hippo definitely ranked higher on the scariness scale.

All he wanted was for Razi and Shifa to be well on the way. He tried to send out a silent message to them. *Marco is coming and he'll stop at nothing. Please hurry.*

# Chapter Eighteen

Soon Razi and Shifa had left the whales behind as they moved on in search of the islet. Razi sniffled and wrapped himself up tightly in the sack. Even covered up like that he dried off pretty quickly in the sun.

"All right now, Razi?" asked Shifa.

Razi nodded. "Hey, look! There's the islet."

Two more blue whales frolicked in the distance, keeping out of their way. Razi swapped places with Shifa and rowed toward the islet. Now that they were closer they could see it was a tiny one, with coconut trees sprouting all over it and a rocky cliff on one side. Razi steered around it first, giving it a wide berth until they found a suitable landing place. A wide beach on the other side of the cliff made landing perfectly easy.

"It's lovely," said Shifa. "Do you think it's the right one?"

"It has to be."

Razi brought the boat in and Shifa jumped into the water. They pushed the boat up the beach, Razi wedging it safely so that it didn't get carried back out.

The island was circular and sandy. There was a small clearing near the cliff, and a few rocky parts, but other than that it was quite uninteresting.

Razi spread out the map on a large flat rock and held it down to keep it from flapping. They bent over it, squinting at the islet.

"This is definitely the place," said Razi. "Look at this." He pointed to some jagged markings. "Doesn't that look like the cliff?"

"Yes!" Shifa looked around her in excitement. "So the X is somewhere on this side."

Razi considered the map and turned it around so that the cliff on the map pointed to the real cliff. "Something's wrong, though."

Shifa nodded and sat back on her heels. She held her hair back as it flapped over her face.

The map showed an oval landmark with ridges running through it, but nothing of the sort corresponded to anything they could see. The *X* marking the treasure was right next to the oval, almost touching it, in fact. Razi and Shifa were silent as they tried to process what this meant.

"Do you think we're on the wrong islet?" said Shifa at last.

Razi shrugged. "It *has* to be the right one, doesn't it? There's no other single islet around here, and the map doesn't show any other land other than little clusters of islets in twos or threes. We can't see anything for miles around here."

Shifa stared at the map, as if willing it to reveal the answers.

"Do you think whatever that oval is supposed to be could have been destroyed?" said Razi. "Some sort of natural event—I don't know, erosion or rust or something." Even as he said it, it sounded unlikely.

"Whatever it is, it looks quite big, though. I mean, when you look at it in proportion to the size of the islet, it's not *tiny*. I can't think how it could be gone without leaving some trace behind. Also, didn't Zheng say that the treasure was only buried weeks ago? That's a very short time for something to disappear without a trace."

"Should we just dig anyway? All around this area?" Razi stroked a part of the map with his finger. He was itching to get going. The sooner they found the treasure, the quicker they could save Zheng before something happened to him.

"We could." Shifa was hesitant. She turned around slowly, taking in the whole space.

Razi sighed under his breath. It would be a lot of digging. They had no idea how deep it had been buried either. There was no way they could do all that.

Razi felt like screaming. The clock was ticking and they had no idea how close the two men were to finding the islet. What were they missing? Something crucial was wrong in the map. He looked at the elongated oval shape on the map again, noticing the seven ridges running along it lengthwise.

Razi paused. "There's something about this." He looked at Shifa. "I feel like I've seen it before. Have you?"

Shifa considered it for a long time. "I don't think so."

But he couldn't shake off the feeling that it was familiar. Something he'd seen before.

"Maybe there's another clue in the map," said Shifa. They examined it again, holding it down on the hot rock so that it didn't flutter away. "What about the sun on the side there, casting rays?"

Razi frowned. "That's just to show direction, I think. It's showing that that side's east."

"Hmm, I don't know. It's more normal to show north in a map, isn't it? Why show east?"

"Good point." He wondered if Zheng had any clues from the captain that could help. Something flickered on the edges of his memory, but he couldn't quite catch hold of it.

"This is hopeless," said Shifa, looking up. "Not much can change in a matter of weeks. Maybe we've got it wrong. Or maybe there never was a Dagger of Serendib here. Either way, there's nothing we can do now. We should leave."

"No! Without the treasure, we'd have nothing to bargain with. What about Zheng? What about taking the dagger back home where it belongs!"

"We're too exposed out here. We agreed we'd be back home before nightfall. If Marco and Cook get here, we're finished."

"But if we leave, then *Zheng's* finished."

Shifa stared around helplessly. "I know, but we can't help him if we get caught. We'll have to think of something else, Razi."

As if in response to her mood, Razi sensed a change in the atmosphere. The sky darkened suddenly and the wind dropped. Razi stared at the sea as Shifa rolled up the map and put it in its lotus-leaf case.

A chill settled in his heart as everything went a dull gray.

"What's the matter?" said Shifa. "Come on! We should leave before Marco gets here."

Razi cleared his throat. "I don't mean to scare you, but we couldn't leave even if we wanted to."

# Chapter Nineteen

"What are you talking about?" Shifa stared at him. "Of course we can leave. We have to."

"It's just that I think it would be advisable to stay, that's all. Let's not overthink these things; best to just go with the flow. Now, where shall we—"

"Razi, stop blabbering! I can tell you're scared to death. What's the matter?"

He looked at his sister. "There's a storm coming."

"All the more reason to get out of here at once," said Shifa, running to the boat.

"No! We can't go to sea like this. Look at that sky! It's madness."

"It was fine two minutes ago!" shouted Shifa. She looked panicked. "Which means it must be miles away and moving really slowly. We'll just have to row fast and get back quickly."

"Shifa, it's too dangerous," he said. "We'll have to stay on the islet tonight."

A flash in the sky made them jump. Then there was a clap of thunder and Shifa screamed.

"We can't stay on this islet during a storm! We just can't, Razi. Let's get out right now so that we beat it."

But Razi was shaking his head even as she was speaking.

"Are you sure?" she said. "I mean—"

"I'm positive. I'm a fisherboy, Shifa. I know how to read the sea."

His sister took a deep breath. "You're right." Her eyes were red, as if she was trying hard not to cry. "It's just—this—" She gestured around them at the little islet, small and unprotected. "I really don't want to be stuck here in the middle of the ocean during a storm."

Razi looked around them and the seriousness of the situation sank in. How big was the storm? What if the islet got submerged? "We should secure the boat," he said.

They ran to the boat and dragged it farther up the beach, being careful not to damage it.

"Let's get it right to the middle, close to the cliff," said Razi. "Then there's less chance it could get swept out to sea."

He really wasn't sure what to expect.

"It's just a precaution. I don't think we need to worry," he lied.

Shifa didn't look convinced but she helped bring in the boat and wedge it under the cliff in a copse of coconut trees. Razi secured it by lashing it to one of the trees. In a storm where even the thickest tree could fall he knew the wiry coconut tree was the strongest of all. He triple-tied it, hoping it was enough to secure their lifeline.

Then he looked out to sea in disbelief. "Oh no! It's Marco!"

They ran to the shore. Sure enough, Marco and Cook were coming toward them at speed in a fancy-looking boat. What was he playing at? He had to know about the storm!

"What do we do?" said Razi, panicking. He took the map from Shifa and put it down his shirt like Zheng had done.

"Let's be bold about it," she said. "We can't run away so let's pretend we're not scared."

As the boat got closer they could see there was another figure slumped down inside.

"Zheng!" said Shifa, practically squealing with happiness. "He's alive!"

Zheng was bound and gagged, bouncing around in the boat as they came nearer. His eyes widened at the sight of Razi and Shifa and he shook his head from side to side.

"Too late, Zheng," said Razi under his breath. "We're here now." But his heart was soaring at the sight of the boy.

The boat landed and Marco jumped out. "Where is it?" he said, barreling toward the children.

Cook brought the boat up and jumped out too. Zheng was left in the boat, wriggling and protesting through his gag.

"Where is what?" asked Razi.

"Don't play games with me," said Marco, his voice dangerously icy.

"You can have the map," said Shifa. "But please let Zheng go."

Marco gave a mirthless laugh. "Nice try. We don't need the map now. Where's the treasure?"

"We couldn't find it," said Razi. "We did try."

He glanced up at the dark clouds, now stacking up vertically overhead. Marco looked up too, and his expression darkened.

Cook and Marco shared a look. Razi knew they were thinking about the storm.

"Where's your boat?" Marco asked suddenly, looking around.

Shifa answered in a beat. "The sea was rough and our boat got pulled out."

Marco looked startled, then guffawed loudly.

"We need to go now," said Cook, glancing at the sea. "This boat should just about get us back before the storm hits."

Marco gave them a triumphant look. "That's a good plan, actually. Goodbye, children. Enjoy the storm. We'll be back to get the treasure when it—and you—have gone."

He turned and went up to the boat, Cook jumping in after him. Zheng groaned and flipped around like a fish out of water. To Razi's surprise, Shifa screamed and ran up to the boat behind them.

"This is all your fault!" she said, jumping in and slapping Zheng's face. He looked completely confused as Shifa crouched over him. "We *never* should have got mixed up in any of this."

Marco grabbed her and pushed her off the boat. They sailed quickly away from the islet as the sky got blacker and blacker.

"What are they doing?" said Shifa, stumbling back to Razi, who looked at her, openmouthed. He knew she was frustrated but he'd never seen her do anything like that before. "They're going the wrong way, aren't they?"

"They know the storm is nearly here, so I expect they're going to wait it out somewhere else rather than go all the way back to Serendib."

From their direction, Razi guessed they were trying to land in one of the clusters of islands to the southwest. Somewhere the land was higher perhaps, where they were more protected and sure of being safe. Unlike their tiny, exposed treasure islet.

Despite Shifa's outburst, she didn't seem to have taken in the full implication of Marco's words and he didn't want to make it worse by telling her that, in reality, Marco had left them there to die.

# Chapter Twenty

Thunder crashed overhead.

"Come on," said Razi. "Let's try to find find some shelter."

"The only place is the boat," said Shifa. "The coconut trees might help keep it safe?"

But Razi wasn't so sure. He suddenly had a brain wave. "Let's go up to the cliff."

"What? That's completely exposed."

Razi looked at Shifa. He needed her to grasp the seriousness of the situation.

"I'm worried that the islet will submerge in the storm."

Shifa's normally rosy complexion drained of color. "What, r-really? Okay, let's go up the cliff then."

Thunder growled again, and a sprinkle of rain started to fall. Shifa ran to the boat and grabbed a few items from the basket. "Might as well have some food with us." She stashed the basket back and covered it with a waterproof sheet from the boat.

Razi stuffed the food in his pockets as they went up the cliff. He was glad they hadn't waited for the rain to come bucketing down; it was slippery enough as it was.

Shifa went in front and Razi followed, using the same footholds that she did. The map inside his shirt slipped and he caught it before it fell out. He climbed the last part very quickly, the map in his hand, and just reached the top as lightning flashed, framing him for a second.

The view from the cliff was spectacular. The islet stretched below around them, all grayed out in the haze. The sea, too, had gone gray and almost glassy. Not a single sea creature could be seen. They'd probably all gone into deep water in readiness for the storm.

Razi noticed that the waves hitting the rocks at the edge of the islet were getting stronger and more frequent. The wind was picking up and the coconut leaves started to thrash around.

The children sat under a small overhang in the cliff that gave them a little protection. Opposite, a clump of trees reached high toward the sky.

"That's good," said Shifa. "If lightning strikes it'll do it there!"

"Let's eat," said Razi, giving her a couple of mangosteens from his pocket. "Before everything gets wet."

He took one himself and removed the stalk, crushing the shell between his palms. He took out a couple of the white segments and popped them in his mouth, enjoying their sweetness.

"We'll be all right," said Shifa, as if to convince herself.

Razi pulled out the now slightly crumpled map and pushed it into a long crevice in the cliff behind them. "Of course we will. And look on the bright side. We know that Zheng is alive and well, and we'll rescue him once we're out of this."

It was the only comforting thought as they waited for the coming storm, alone and unprotected in the wide gray ocean.

Zheng's head was sore from having hit it repeatedly on the side of the boat. He maneuvered himself slightly so that he was in a better position to carry out his plan. He had very limited time in which to do what he had to do. The islet was disappearing from view already.

"Southwest," said Cook to Marco, looking at the crumpled copy of the map that Razi had drawn.

Zheng was as surprised as anything when the usually measured Shifa had attacked him like that. Until he felt the coldness of a knife blade press against his hand and he closed his fist around the handle before Marco had thrown her off the boat.

He'd sawed quickly through his ropes but left the gag on. The men were busy trying to get away as fast as they could and hadn't noticed a thing. As soon as he was free, Zheng threw the ropes into the water and jumped in himself.

Cook yelled, "Idiot boy! What's he doing?"

The sea around Zheng churned and spat angrily. He dived under the boat and bobbed up on the other side.

"Leave him!" said Marco. "We don't have time for this. Let him die."

The men thought he was still tied up, seeing only his gagged head in the waves. That suited Zheng fine. He went down again, staying in the murky, churning depths until he was sure the boat had continued on its way.

He popped up and gasped for air. He pulled off the gag quickly and swam toward the islet, which he could hardly see in the hazy grayness. He'd have to be as fast as he could, and keep the islet in sight always.

He was starting to tire before he'd covered even half the distance.

The rain came down quite suddenly and the sound drummed in his ears. He looked around him and realized he'd lost any sense of where the islet was. He'd have to keep swimming and hope for the best.

This was nothing new to Zheng, of course. He was good at keeping his wits about him. The captain had always said that.

The thought of the captain made Zheng's heart contract. From the lonely coldness of his uncle's house he'd found love and belonging on the seas. Now here he was, stuck in the ocean in a storm with no one to miss him if he died.

Zheng slipped under the water.

Nobody would care. Nobody would care if he died.

Except, on a little islet somewhere in the same ocean, there were two children who *did* care.

They cared enough to come for him, leaving behind the safety of their home and a mother who loved them.

Zheng opened his eyes underwater. It was dark and murky down there, just like his insides. A large leatherback turtle swept away in front of him, its distinct markings jogging a memory somewhere. The captain's words came into his mind. *Follow the turtle, Zheng.*

Zheng kicked up and broke the surface.

This time he could make out something in the distance. The cliffs of the islet perhaps? He couldn't give up now.

He was Zheng, survivor of everything!

He struck out with renewed determination and swam toward the cliffs. It was slow going and his arms and legs began to strain. The cliffs got closer, and he could see the islet shrouded in a veil of slashing rain and gray sludge.

He was so close now he could even see the beach in front of him. But exhaustion had overtaken his body and his vision had gone blurry.

"Razi!" he called out, his voice feeble and drowned out by the crashing waves. "Shifa!" He had to stay conscious. He tried to take in deep breaths but sputtered from inhaling rain and seawater.

Despite his determination, he could feel himself losing the battle and closed his eyes.

# Chapter Twenty-One

When the rain came, it lashed down in curtains, drumming into the cliff and drenching the little islet. Razi and his sister huddled close together, pressing into the overhang as much as they could, sometimes clinging on as the wind raged and slashed at them. They were soon cold, wet, and hungry, and the rain poured relentlessly around them, pooling at their feet and preventing them from moving.

At the foot of the cliff, the boat

juddered violently as the wind battered it. The coconut trunks seemed to be forming a protective cage around it. The island had begun to submerge, but only just, and the boat bobbed in place as the ropes held.

After some time, the wind ceased, leaving a steady drumming of rain and a sense of peace.

Razi shifted and stretched a little. His limbs felt stiff and his palms stung from clinging on to the rock. "Are you okay, Shifa? I think the worst has passed."

Shifa nodded, water dripping off the end of her nose. "I hope Zheng's all right, wherever he is."

"They're experienced seamen. I'm sure Marco would have made it to shelter in time, so he'll be fine."

"I hope you're right." After a pause Shifa said, "Are *you* okay?"

Razi watched the raindrops pelting into the sea, forming little tumblers of water around each.

"I was wondering about earlier...," said Shifa. "You're not afraid of the water anymore. Are you?"

The rain pattered down around them as Razi struggled with how to explain. "I was never afraid of the water."

Shifa turned to him, listening.

"I-I don't know how to describe it. I wasn't afraid

of the sea. I didn't think I was in any danger. I just...
disliked it. Intensely."

He thought she might find that odd, but she didn't.

"And?" she said.

"And when I finally went back in the water and saw
the whales today, I realized how much I had missed it.
How happy it made me."

He had forgiven the sea. There'd be no more Father.
There, he'd said it. Father was never coming back. It
was time for life to go on without him, and to go back to
the thing that had taken him away.

# Chapter Twenty-Two

The storm petered out later that evening, leaving everything dripping and sodden. Razi had no idea how long they'd been there. He stood up and stretched. The sun had dipped too, leaving a trail of stippled oranges and purples on the horizon. The water had receded from the islet and the boat was once again resting on the sand beneath the coconut trees.

Razi sneezed. His fingers were shriveled up like namnam fruit.

"Come on," said Shifa. She was making her way carefully down the cliff. "Let's see if there are any dry clothes."

"Coming." He picked his way down to the boat, where Shifa had already gotten the basket out from under the waterproof sheet and found it was mercifully dry.

"We need to get changed," she said. "But I can't find a single dry spot of ground anywhere."

In the end they sat in the boat for the night, even though not much of it had escaped the rains. The night was dark but everything was bathed in moonlight.

Razi found the last remaining mangosteens and some crispy rosette cakes that were squashed at the bottom of the basket with a few slabs of sesame toffee.

"We should leave as soon as possible in the morning," said Shifa. "Before Marco comes back. We'll need a new plan after that."

The rosettes were crispy and sweet, and Razi crumpled a whole one into his mouth. He didn't like the idea of leaving without the treasure. But Shifa was right. They couldn't rescue Zheng here. "We'll leave first thing."

They curled up on either side of the boat, looking up at the stars through the trailing canopy of coconut branches.

Razi closed his eyes and tried to sleep. He knew there was something familiar about that oval shape on the map, something that blurred at the edge of his mind and wouldn't become clear. But no matter how hard he puzzled, he couldn't work out what it was, and the frustration of being so close to the treasure and yet so far from finding it kept him awake long after Shifa had fallen into a deep, exhausted sleep.

# Chapter Twenty-Three

The sound of egrets squawking overhead woke Razi the next day. Tiny fingers of daylight crept through the canopy of branches, and waves slapped hard against the rocks. Shifa was still sleeping, her head resting on the side of the boat. A brand-new day was dawning, as if the storm had never happened at all.

He shook Shifa awake. "Come on. Let's take the boat to the back of the island this time," said Razi. "There's a small stretch of beach there that we can leave from, and it's covered by the cliff too. If Marco were to come the same way as yesterday he wouldn't see it."

Shifa took out the basket, spade, and waterproof sheet to reduce the weight and together they struggled around the island with the boat and moored it with the rope.

Razi looked out to sea, squinting against the just-rising sun. The sea sparkled in silvery blue, and a large turtle was making her way up the beach. Razi ran down to meet her, the salty spray waking him up at once.

The turtle was massive, the length of a grown man. She had a thick wizened head and a black leathery shell. She fluffed the sand as she walked up the beach with her rubbery front flippers.

"Hello, hello!" Razi walked beside her up the beach. "I'm Razi, what's your name?"

The turtle ignored him and settled down on the sand, where she lay sunning herself, occasionally moving her head as if to catch the best rays.

"Looks like you're a regular here then," said Razi, watching her with amusement. The turtle seemed very comfortable.

The islet was bright and vibrant as the sun slowly rose, freshly washed after the storm, all its colors sparkling with a new lease on life.

"The size of that!" Shifa came up behind him, rubbing her eyes. "I've never seen such a thing. Do we have them on Serendib?"

"Yes, she's a leatherback turtle." Razi pointed to the ridges on her back. "There are loads on Serendib if you'd ever just come down to the sea and look. See, she has a rubbery shell, not the hard type like the other turtles."

Shifa shrugged. "Come on, Razi, let's get going. We'll eat on the way."

Razi went off to wash himself in the sea. As he approached the shore, he squinted at something on the beach nearby, lying on the flat rock where they'd read the map yesterday. Was that...? His scalp began to prickle.

"Shifa!" he yelled. Razi raced down to the rock. A crumpled figure lay there, wet and encrusted with sand.

Razi stopped short and stifled a scream. It was Zheng. He seemed to be asleep…

Shifa thudded up behind him. With a sharp intake of breath she dropped to her knees and lifted Zheng up by his shoulders.

"Zheng! Zheng, it's us! Look, Zheng! Open your eyes."

She banged on his back with her palm.

Zheng tried to roll away from her but was clearly too weak.

Shifa breathed a sigh of relief and stopped hitting him.

Zheng coughed and opened his eyes slightly and closed them again. Then he opened them fully and stared at something over Shifa's shoulder.

"Let's get him to the boat," Shifa said to Razi. "We have to get out of here fast."

Razi jumped up at once.

"No," said Zheng hoarsely. He pointed behind Shifa and tried to say something else. He looked weak and exhausted.

"It's okay, Zheng," said Shifa. "We'll talk in the boat on the way back. We have to leave now."

Zheng shook his head violently. His eyes were glazed and unfocused. He pointed again and again and said something unintelligible.

Razi put Zheng's arm over his neck so he could help him to the boat. The boy resisted at once.

"Follow the turtle," Zheng croaked.

Razi paused, gobsmacked. "What did he say? *Follow the turtle?*"

Shifa shrugged. "He must be delirious. Quick, let's get him to the boat."

But Zheng wouldn't move and kept pointing to the turtle. He rasped something that sounded like *follow* again.

"We don't have time for this," said Shifa, looking panic-stricken at the sea. "They might come back any minute now that it's light."

"I left the map on the cliff! I'll have to go and get it."

"Oh, Razi, you idiot!" cried Shifa. "Please hurry. And see if you can see Marco's boat while you're up there."

Razi hurried up the cliff as fast as he could. He found the map where he'd left it the previous evening. It was perfectly dry, protected as it was in Shifa's case and nestling safely in the crevice. He went to the edge of the cliff and looked out over the horizon for Marco. But there was no sign of anyone.

He could see Shifa kneeling next to Zheng on the beach. The sea roared and white-crested waves raced in and out just by their feet. The giant turtle rested off to the side, the ridges on her back glinting in the morning sun. In the water now and then a whale surfaced, with its booming deepwater sound, shooting out jets of water high into the air. Pods of dolphins vaulted in curving arcs, soaring and splashing in an endless display.

Razi's breath caught in his throat. He'd seen something amazing. Something hidden in plain sight. The thing they'd been looking for all this time.

He took out the map and opened it, holding it up next to the scene in front of him.

It matched perfectly.

And just like that, everything cleared in Razi's mind.

He knew exactly where the treasure was.

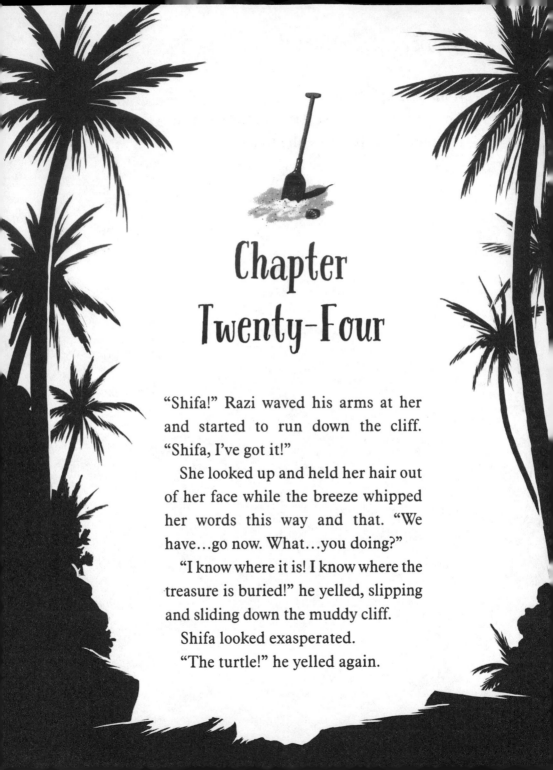

# Chapter Twenty-Four

"Shifa!" Razi waved his arms at her and started to run down the cliff. "Shifa, I've got it!"

She looked up and held her hair out of her face while the breeze whipped her words this way and that. "We have…go now. What…you doing?"

"I know where it is! I know where the treasure is buried!" he yelled, slipping and sliding down the muddy cliff.

Shifa looked exasperated.

"The turtle!" he yelled again.

Razi hurtled to a stop in front of his sister and held up the map with shaking hands.

It was all as clear as daylight. The oval-shaped object on the map was on the beach now. The elongated shape and the seven ridges on the turtle's back perfectly mimicked the pattern on the shape in the map.

Shifa gasped. "The landmark was a moving one! A turtle."

"That's what Zheng was trying to tell us!"

They looked at Zheng, lying on the beach. "Finally," he croaked. He bent over and coughed up some water.

After he'd fetched the spade, Razi helped Zheng to where the turtle was. Zheng was looking much better from earlier, though still very quiet.

The turtle continued basking in the sun, completely ignoring the children.

"Er, what do we do now?" said Shifa. "We need her to move."

Razi scratched his head. The turtle was massive, weighing as much as ten men.

"Could we give her a little nudge?" said Shifa. "Just to encourage her to move. I'm all for letting her enjoy her daily ritual, but it *is* a matter of life and death that we get out of here fast."

"No, no nudges," said Razi. "I think they bite. They have really strong jaws."

"That settles it then," she said. "We'll wait."

"Well, the boat is ready to sail. As soon as she leaves we dig for the treasure and run. If Marco comes before that, we run too. And maybe come back once he's off our backs."

"I can't believe this," said Shifa. "If we weren't here at sunrise we would have missed everything."

"You know, the rising sun in the map," said Razi. "*That's* what it was indicating. That the map is right at sunrise."

Zheng nodded. "I think..." he said, still a little hoarse, "I think the turtle comes here every sunrise and leaves after a while."

"And the captain's words to you!" said Razi. "*Follow the turtle, it leads you to good things.* He meant it quite literally!"

Zheng gave a sad smile.

"How did the captain know that the turtle would keep coming back to this same spot? What if she settled on a different place? What if she stopped coming?"

"He was born around here, wasn't he?" said Razi. "Maybe he'd seen her before. And we don't know much about turtles. I mean, they somehow come back to the same beach to lay their eggs as much as twenty years after leaving as newborns. Or maybe *this* particular one is a creature of habit and the captain knew it. They do live a long time too, so he guessed she'd keep coming and be a good marker for the treasure. Who would ever think that's what the map showed?"

"Yes," said Zheng. His face had regained some of his usual animation, and he seemed to be getting his voice back too. "I think this one was coming here during the captain's childhood, and when he saw her when he came with the treasure he must have gotten the idea to bury it in her spot."

Razi stared admiringly at the leatherback, a living marker for one of Serendib's most prized possessions.

The turtle started to move off back to the sea. Razi couldn't be sure but he thought she looked annoyed. He couldn't blame her; she'd wanted a bit of peace and quiet and here they were having a whole conversation over her head.

Razi struck the ground with the spade as soon as she'd left.

The sand was damp and clumpy and Razi had to dig hard. While he worked, Zheng explained how he'd escaped from Marco. Razi looked with admiration at his sister when Zheng got to the part about the knife. Shifa shrugged as if she did such things every day.

"You've had the most awful time, Zheng," said Razi, digging hard.

"Tell me about it," said Zheng. "And you know the worst part? I was gagged and so for hours and hours I couldn't *talk*."

Razi and Shifa stared at Zheng, not sure if he was joking. Zheng was making outraged gestures as if he were deadly serious.

The sand was soft and yielding, and the spade slid easily through it. While Razi worked, he and Shifa updated Zheng about their adventures, about fighting off Marco and about Maalu. Soon he was standing in a mound of sand. How far down could the treasure be? His arms were starting to hurt but he kept digging furiously.

And then the spade hit something.

"Yes!" exclaimed Zheng, peering into the hole. "This is *exactly* how I felt when we unearthed a sultana's hidden diadem too…"

Razi's arms were trembling with excitement now. He jumped into the hole and touched the bottom. Something was there. He pulled the spade in and dug some more. There was definitely something hard in the sand.

He moved the packed sand away with the spade, digging down the sides to reveal a small box about two handspans in size. Shifa and Zheng jumped in after him and they all dug around the box with their bare hands.

It was hard work getting the box out but eventually Razi lifted it out of the hole and laid it on the ground.

The captain's treasure chest stared back at them.

# Chapter Twenty-Five

The three of them looked at each other and broke into peals of laughter.

"We did it!" said Zheng, grasping Razi and Shifa and pulling them into a happy jig.

"Let's look inside," said Razi, scraping off a layer of sand on top with his fingers. Shifa blew off the rest, revealing an intricately carved lid.

"That's pretty," said Shifa, as Razi slid his fingers under the lid to pry it open.

Zheng looked on with a faraway expression.

It was a square wooden box of teak, thick and well made, with beautiful lotus carvings on the top.

The lid wouldn't move. Razi tried to lift it but it wouldn't budge.

"Maybe it slides off," said Zheng. He pushed the lid sideway and it moved stiffly, chunks of sand falling inside as it opened.

Before it was even fully off they could see that this was the captain's hidden treasure.

It was the Dagger of Serendib, the hilt carved and topped by a roaring lion head, now tarnished by time. Razi lifted it carefully out of the box. There was something emotional about seeing it, in spite of its dullness, as if they were handling a living piece of history. Razi passed it to Shifa to see.

The rest of the box was full of roughly shaped coins and a few small trinkets. Zheng scooped up a handful and examined them.

A scuffle behind him made Razi start, and Zheng dropped the coins he was holding.

"There they are!"

Razi yelled as Marco knocked him out of the way. They'd been so engrossed in the treasure they'd forgotten to look out for the men.

Shifa put the dagger roughly into the box and slammed the lid shut. She picked up the box but Marco snatched it out of her hands.

"So you pests survived," said Marco, cradling the box greedily. He stared at Zheng. "You! How did you get here?"

Cook smirked as he came up behind him. "We should be thanking them. They've done all the work for us."

Marco tried to open the box's lid but couldn't pry it off so just held it under his arm.

Suddenly Razi jumped on Marco and tried to wrestle the box out of his hands, but Cook grabbed him by the back of his shirt and pulled him off.

Marco pounced on Zheng. "Well, what a great thing this is!" he said, dragging a squirming Zheng away with one hand, the box tucked under the other arm.

Cook held Razi and Shifa back but Shifa broke free and ran after Marco.

"Fine, you can keep it!" she yelled. "But leave Zheng. You've got what you wanted."

The man stopped for a moment and laughed. "I don't think so. He's caused us an awful lot of trouble and needs to be punished for getting in our way."

"You can't do that!" said Razi. If the men left now, that would be it. They wouldn't have a clue where they'd take Zheng or what they'd do with him.

"And by the way." Marco turned back suddenly, leaving Zheng gasping in his grip. "If I see you two interfering *one more time*, I'm going to kill you. Understand?"

Razi stared at him, thinking. He knew the real reason Marco was leaving them there. The men, powerfully built as they were, knew they couldn't control three struggling children. And Marco thought they'd lost their boat, so they couldn't raise the alarm or even leave the island. They'd have to be rescued, by which time the two men would be long gone.

Razi turned back to Shifa and tried to send her a message with his eyes. Cook looked at him suspiciously, wondering why he'd given up.

Razi glanced toward their boat, lying ready in the sea and hidden by the cliffs. Then he threw back his head and yelled, kicking and punching Cook. Out of the corner of his eye, he saw Shifa slip silently away while Cook was distracted.

He gave her a few minutes and then he broke free from Cook and ran at Marco hard. He jumped onto his shoulders. At the same time Zheng bit down viciously on Marco's hand as Cook raced to help his friend.

Marco yelled and dropped the box. Razi scooped it up and sprinted away. Zheng got away from Marco, only to be grabbed again by Cook.

Marco and Cook stopped and watched Razi run away, bemused. "What are the fools doing now?" said Marco. "They can't get away without a boat. Idiots."

Razi waded into the water and threw the box into the boat. He jumped in quickly as Shifa rowed off. "Zheng's still caught," he called to her. "We have to do something."

They moved quickly around the island, enjoying seeing Marco and Cook's enraged faces as they realized what was happening.

The men threw themselves and a protesting Zheng into their boat and gave chase.

"Take over, Razi," said Shifa, jumping out of her seat.

Razi slid in and rowed hard, his arms moving like a machine, faster and faster.

"Give us Zheng," Shifa yelled across the water. "And we'll give you the box."

Marco grimaced and pulled harder on his boat. Theirs was a modern contraption in these parts. All sleek and smart, not like the traditional fishing boats Razi was used to, the ones his grandfather and great-grandfather had used before them. They made a terrible getaway vehicle.

Razi knew the men wouldn't just hand Zheng over. He and Shifa would have to be very clever and sneaky.

On the open seas Marco and Cook had everything over them. They were closing in all the time. Nathan's little fishing boat just couldn't keep far enough ahead of them.

Suddenly Marco's boat bumped theirs hard, making them rock violently and nearly toppling Razi out. The box slid down toward the far end of the boat.

"Stop that!" shouted Shifa. "We said we'd give you the box. Just hand Zheng over."

"Give us the box first," said Marco, holding out his hands.

"No," shouted Razi, rowing away from the men as their boat crept nearer. "Don't do it, Shifa! They're trying to trick us."

Cook seemed to be tiring of holding down a wriggling Zheng. "Let's get rid of this wastrel. He's not worth the effort."

Razi held his breath. They wouldn't really do it, would they?

But to Razi's utter shock and dismay Marco flicked a hand, and Cook threw Zheng overboard.

Zheng fell into the water with a surprised "Oh!"

Shifa and Razi were frozen with shock and just stared at the spot in the water where Zheng had disappeared.

Suddenly, from the depths, came a *throb, throb, throb,* and a great gush of water showered the air. It was Maalu!

She gave Razi's boat a friendly bump that shunted it backward into Marco's, knocking him off his feet. Marco swore and picked up a spade from the bottom of the boat, slapping it at Maalu to chase her away.

"WHAT ARE YOU DOING!" Razi screamed.

Maalu keened in pain and disappeared below the surface.

Enraged, Razi grabbed his own spade, intending to beat Marco with it.

"How dare you, you monster!" yelled Shifa. Then Marco reached in and dragged her right out of the boat and into his.

Razi immediately threw down the spade and leaped after her. Nathan's boat bobbed out from under him and began to float away.

Marco let go of Shifa and grabbed Razi. He picked up the spade he'd struck Maalu with and swung it at the boy. Shifa screamed and shoved the big man hard, sending him smacking down onto the deck.

Cook got up and cuffed Razi on his head. He held him down while Marco wrestled Shifa into a headlock. Shifa clawed at his arm but he was too strong.

"Where's the dagger?" yelled Marco.

"Don't hurt her!" screamed Razi. "It's on the boat. Let her go!"

Cook and Marco looked to where Nathan's boat was now drifting away into the blue distance.

Marco suddenly exploded in anger, spit flying all over the place. "YOU KIDS! You have brought me nothing but trouble." He tightened his arm and Shifa spluttered. Razi yelled and kicked out at Cook as he struggled to free himself.

Shifa was in serious danger but she'd managed to pull something from her pocket. Razi couldn't see what it was as he strained against Cook, kicking and screaming as he tried to reach her.

Suddenly, Shifa drew her hand quickly down Marco's face and he let go of her and staggered back, clutching his cheek. Cook rushed to help him.

"That'll teach you to pick on children!" yelled Shifa, backing away and rubbing her neck. "Come on, Razi, we've got a boat to catch."

She grabbed her brother's hand and together they jumped into the sea.

# Chapter Twenty-Six

The two children watched as the men chased after Nathan's boat, Marco groaning and writhing in the back.

"Shifa!" Razi treaded water next to her. "Are you okay?"

"Yes, I'm fine!" sputtered Shifa. "We've got to get on our boat and find Zheng."

"I'm here!" came a voice from behind them. Razi and Shifa gasped in amazement as Zheng swam up to them. "You two took your time," he said. "I was beginning to think I'd have to save the day by myself. Look, they're almost at the boat."

"Good to see you too, Zheng," said Razi, giving his friend a gentle thump on the shoulder.

Zheng beamed.

"Come on!" he cried, striking out after the men.

"What did you do to Marco?" shouted Razi as he and Shifa began swimming after him.

"I had that prickly pear leaf in my pocket. Cut myself on it, too, but it did the trick," Shifa panted. "Don't worry, it only gave him a scratch."

Razi couldn't care less. Trust Shifa to worry about a person who'd nearly killed her.

Zheng was swimming strongly but Nathan's boat was still far out of reach. Razi and Shifa were way behind.

They were in deep trouble. They were *literally* in deep trouble.

Then they felt that now familiar rhythm from the deep again and Maalu appeared out of nowhere, gliding with speed through the water toward the men. As the children watched she slid directly under their boat and breached.

The children gasped as the boat flew up into the air and Maalu thwacked back into the ocean. Marco and Cook were thrown out like rag dolls and the boat smashed back into the sea with a massive thud. It landed well away from its capsized passengers.

Maalu had got her own revenge on Marco.

Razi was shaking in terror. What would happen to them now? Shifa looked ready to pass out. "We'll be okay," she said. "We need to be calm and think."

Razi gulped. There was no land near enough to swim to. Both the boats were far out of reach. They were alone in the deep sea where fishermen rarely ventured.

Razi looked around suddenly. "Where's Zheng?"

Shifa's hair was plastered down over her face and she was shivering. "H-he was somewhere up ahead. I thought I saw a head before."

But the sea around them was empty. All they could see was more and more water lapping endlessly around them. No sign of the two men either. All around was just blue sparkling sea, the sound of whale song, and the splash of dolphins.

Razi plunged down into the ocean and looked around its blurred depths. Far below him on the seabed the corals reached up in tentacles of red and buds of thorny mauve. The hair on his back rose as a creepy sensation overwhelmed him. The ocean inside and outside was hauntingly lonely.

Maalu was coming toward them now, gliding through the water as if to see what they thought of her shenanigans with Marco.

Razi surfaced and called out, "Zheng!"

A few yards away Shifa was shouting for Zheng too.

Razi took a deep breath and plunged back under the surface. Opening his eyes again, he noticed a hazy, undulating shadow coming toward him. He put out his hand. *Krill*. The little fish that whales ate. There was a massive shoal of them in front of him.

Then suddenly he was in the middle of it.

The sea went dark as a huge shape blotted out the light. Maalu! A cold fear gripped him. She was thundering toward him, on her side and mouth wide open, scooping up the krill.

Razi froze in terror.

*Whales don't eat people. Whales don't eat people. Whales don't eat people!* He repeated it over and over but she was coming toward him so fast he was hypnotized. What an end to his life! Maalu powered toward him and Razi felt her jaws close around his body and a crushing pain pressed down on his hips.

He was caught in the mouth of the largest animal ever.

# Chapter Twenty-Seven

*The ocean and the sky were the same brilliant blue, both bleeding into each other and blending as one. Zheng felt the wind hum past him, cool and refreshing, as he flew through the water on the back of the whale. Someone was sitting behind him. He looked around and saw it was Shifa, laughing in glee as they skimmed through the waves.*

*Zheng looked around in astonishment. This couldn't be real. Sure, he'd been on a lot of adventures, but this one was unparalleled. Even for him.*

*And where was Razi?*

*Something loomed up in front of them. Zheng squinted into the distance. Was that land? The whale dived down and Zheng grabbed its barnacled body as they plummeted into the depths, then everything went black again.*

Zheng opened his eyes. It was evening and he was lying on a beach, sandy and wet. A wave came in and washed over his legs. The sun was setting over on the other side of the islet.

His chest felt full and heavy. Sand was in his hair, his face, his clothes. Even inside his mouth.

It took him a moment to realize where he was. The islet and cliff top looked bare and lonely.

"Razi! Shifa!" Zheng crawled up the beach and pulled himself up. Terror and grief tore through him at the memory of what had happened. What had he done to his friends?

There was a movement behind him and Zheng ran toward it. Shifa was lying on the beach too, even more sandy and woozy than he was. She sat up and tried to brush the sand out of her eyes.

Zheng knelt down at her side. Relief flooded through him.

"I'm okay," she said, dusting off sand from her hair. "Where's Razi?"

"I-I don't know."

"You don't know?" Shifa got up and called out. "Razi?" She ran around the islet, calling his name. Zheng went up to the cliff to look, but both islet and sea were deserted.

He came down dejectedly. "Last I saw, he was..." Zheng couldn't continue.

Shifa swallowed. A clump of sand fell off her bedragggled hair. "He was dangling out of the mouth of the whale."

Zheng didn't want to think about the rest.

"It must have been an accident," she said. "Maalu's so big and Razi's so small she can't have seen him in the middle of the krill. I thought I would go mad with screaming. I think I saw her spit him out but I feel like I passed out and now I don't know what happened for sure."

"I don't know what happened to me either. Things went strange after that."

Shifa walked through the beach and sat on the flat rock. She shook her head. "How did we get here?"

"You'll never believe it," said Zheng. "We came on the back of a whale."

>>⟩

Razi woke up with a gasp when he slammed into something hard.

He was still in the ocean, but now he found himself clinging semiconsciously on to part of Marco's boat. It was empty and battered but it was still afloat.

Razi hauled himself up and flopped down inside. Where was he, and what was going on? Suddenly everything came back to him and Razi started. Shifa! Where was she? Zheng!

He stared around him wildly. Nothing but empty ocean. Or was it?

"Shifa!" he yelled. "Zheng!"

There was an answering cry and Razi steered the boat straight to where it came from. To his surprise it was Cook, his clothes ballooning out around him.

Without a word Razi helped him into the boat. Cook clambered in heavily, almost pulling Razi back into the water in the process.

The man lay down, completely depleted. He seemed to be in a bad way. Razi ignored him and continued to shout for Shifa and Zheng. But the next person he came across was Marco.

He turned the boat and left him there as Marco called out to him. No way was he going to jeopardize his own life while he was looking for Shifa and Zheng.

Razi hadn't gone more than a few yards before guilt overcame him. Shifa would never act like him. He went back for Marco and hoped he wouldn't regret his actions.

But of course, once Marco was in the boat, he immediately turned it in the direction of Serendib, despite Razi's protestations.

"Get away from me!" he yelled at Razi. His thick, muscular features were stony with rage and disappointment. "Unless you want me to throw you back in the water."

Razi slumped back down. He couldn't fight Marco alone. He stared into the water as the boat sped away and the tears fell as he realized there was no way he would ever find Shifa and Zheng now.

# Chapter Twenty-Eight

"Let's take it one step at a time," said Zheng. "This isn't as bad as it looks."

Shifa sighed. "Yes, I'm sure you've survived eight weeks on a desert island in the company of a scorpion, or were raised by polar bears for six months of your life, so this is *nothing*."

Zheng was a bit put out by her dismissive tone. "You know, Shifa, I'm starting to get the feeling you don't believe the things I say."

Shifa ignored him and went to fill up the hole they'd dug earlier, so that the turtle's rest wouldn't be disturbed.

It was getting dark and Zheng knew they couldn't do much now anyway.

"There's a bit of shelter at the foot of the cliff," said Shifa after a while. "And there's some food we had to leave behind when we were escaping."

Zheng trudged to the piece of ground surrounded by coconut trees where Shifa had spread out a waterproof sheet and was taking some food out of a round-bottomed cane basket.

She handed him some slabs of something he couldn't identify but which tasted delicious.

"Listen, Zheng, I'm sorry about earlier," she said. "I didn't mean to be so dismissive of you. We have to work together if we want to survive."

"I'd like that," said Zheng, nodding. "I'm sorry I've annoyed you with my stories. It's so tiresome to have led such an exciting life."

Shifa burst out laughing. "Don't worry, Zheng, and please never change."

The stars twinkled overhead as the sound of the waves washed comfortingly around them. "I think Razi is very lucky to have a sister like you. It's something I never had."

Shifa smiled. She actually looked a little overcome.

"You can consider me the sister you never had then. After all, you do irritate me like a true sibling."

Zheng laughed. They went to sleep soon after the meal, curling up at either end of the sheltered ground.

His heart hurt him, but not with sadness. He thought he'd lost the only family he'd ever known, but it looked like it was always possible to find a new one.

Early the next morning Zheng was awoken by the sound of cormorants whistling and thrashing around in the water. It was still dark but a sliver of light was coming over the horizon. Shifa wasn't there but he heard her moving around on the beach.

He was about to join her when his eyes fell on the few remaining supplies in the basket. Just a few slabs of sesame toffee remained next to a box of matches.

He went out to wash and stopped halfway.

A box of *matches*. They had matches in their basket. Still dry and perfectly usable.

Zheng shouted for Shifa. She was watching the leatherback shuffle up the beach again in its usual dawn ritual.

"Look what we have!" He ran out, shaking the box of matches. "And dry too. We could light a fire. Someone might see it."

"All the way here? Who's going to see it here?"

Zheng shrugged. "It's worth a *try*, don't you think? Smoke rising from the middle of the sea? Someone might come check it out. A boat passing somewhere close by."

Shifa smiled. "Come on." She ran toward the cliff. "Let's build it as high as possible."

Zheng dragged some branches to the top of the cliff and Shifa arranged them carefully, set a match to them and, when the flame caught, she blew gently on it through a tube she'd made with a hollow coconut shell.

Soon a fire was roaring at the top of the cliff, and they stood back to admire it.

"Now what?" said Shifa, looking at the smoke rising into the sky.

"We wait," said Zheng.

By afternoon they were still keeping the fire going but starting to lose hope. They were both beginning to think no one was going to rescue them but neither wanted to say it out loud.

"How long can we keep this up?" said Zheng as he took up another batch of branches.

"As long as it takes." Shifa looked toward the sea. There was nothing there now. The turtle was long gone and even the whales and dolphins had left for the day. "We need to get back home and find Razi."

"Shifa," said Zheng. He shuffled his feet in the hot sand. "There is the possibility you know, that Razi is, er…"

"No," she said simply.

Zheng was about to say something when she interrupted.

"I don't know how to explain it. Razi and I are twins. If…if he was dead, I'd know it."

Zheng nodded. He didn't understand the feeling but it felt true to him.

"What's that?" said Shifa suddenly, getting off the rock and pointing into the distance.

"Where?" Zheng squinted but couldn't see anything.

"There!" Shifa's voice was trembling with excitement. She dashed to the cliff and climbed up.

Zheng got up to follow. Shifa screamed, and her words floated down to him.

"It's a boat! It's a boat, Zheng! Someone's coming to get us."

# Chapter Twenty-Nine

"Thank you," said Shifa for the fourth time since they'd set off.

The man nodded in amusement. He was a fisherman from a village up the beach from them. "I was curious when I saw the fire. It gave me quite a shock. I never expected to be rescuing anyone stranded there."

"We're so glad you did," said Shifa. "My, er, brother and I are very grateful."

Zheng smiled and nodded. Shifa had asked him not to talk at all.

The man seemed a bit skeptical but didn't question it.

"Um, I was wondering." Shifa twisted the end of her hair. "I was just wondering if anyone else had been rescued from the sea recently."

Zheng listened with interest.

"Not that I know of," said the man.

Zheng leaned back in disappointment. It wasn't necessarily bad news, though. The man wouldn't know everything.

"It's funny you should ask," continued the fisherman. "There was a boat that was found drifting in the sea. It was a good thing it was marked with the name. There was a painting of a turtle on the side too."

"Do you, um"—Shifa licked her lips—"do you happen to know what happened to it? The boat, I mean."

"The people who found it returned it, of course. Took it back to the person it belonged to."

"Was there anything in it?" asked Zheng, before he could stop himself. Shifa kicked him in the shin.

The boatman frowned as he rowed up to the shore. "In the boat? I don't know. Why do you ask?"

"Just wondered," answered Shifa for him, and Zheng went back to smiling and nodding again.

He exchanged a look with Shifa behind the boatman's back. *Was the dagger discovered?*

"Just there," said Shifa, pointing to Turtle Beach. "That's where we live, drop us there."

"Are you sure?" said the man. "I didn't think anyone lived here."

"Oh, we do. We like the, er, isolation," said Zheng, before he remembered he wasn't meant to talk.

Shifa glared at Zheng and he was sorry at once. He wished he didn't find it so hard to keep his mouth shut.

"He means the peace and quiet," said Shifa.

The man looked a bit suspicious. "Okay. I can't think why you'd lie so I'm going to drop you off here. Make sure you run off home now. Your family must be worried about you."

They hopped off the boat and splashed into the water, running up to the shore and waving to him. He sat watching for a while so they ran inland, then hid behind a tree, waiting till he rowed away.

"Okay, he's gone," said Shifa. "Let's go to the hut and think about what to do next."

Going into the hut felt like coming home to Zheng. The bundle of clothes that Razi had given him was still in a corner of the room.

"You stay here," said Shifa. "I'm going to slip out to town and see if there's any news of Razi. I can't go home, of course, because Mother would never let me leave, but if…if anything bad's happened I'll find out."

"Okay, I'll be here."

Shifa was gone for a couple of hours. Zheng was starving so he went out and got some King coconuts, breaking them up like Razi had done and eating the inside pulp.

"No luck," said Shifa when she got back. She looked glum and anxious. "There's no sign that Razi's been home but that doesn't mean he's not hiding out somewhere too. Here, I took some food while I was there and left a note for Mother saying we'd be back soon and not to worry."

Zheng took the parcel from her. "You know the boat that Razi and you were using? When did you say the owner was coming back?"

"Two weeks," said Shifa, looking out of the window at the beach.

"So there's a chance the dagger might still be in it! If the fishermen who took it back to Nathan's didn't notice anything."

Shifa turned back from the window. "Yes. And if Razi's here, he might be thinking the same thing." A glint of hope had come into her eyes again.

"Let's go and find the boat!" Zheng got up and bounded to the door.

"Wait! The boats are on the beach right where the fishermen's houses are. We can't go there now without attracting attention. It's going to be dark soon; we'll go then."

# Chapter Thirty

As soon as it was dark Zheng and Shifa set off soundlessly, swishing through the sand in their bare feet. The sea was rough that night, roaring in the moonlight as they walked to Galle.

As they got closer, the bright lamps of the town blinked into view. Coconut palms swayed in their wiry gentleness, flanking the row of modest fishermen's houses facing the beach.

Zheng had a memory of a different part of the world when he saw it.

He felt a pang of homesickness for his previous life, of docking in the most strange and marvelous places and having the most amazing times. The world was so similar and so different at the same time.

"There," whispered Shifa, pointing.

At this time of night all the boats were on the beach. In a few hours the fishermen would come out to go to sea. Zheng could make out the turtle painting on Nathan's boat even in the moonlight.

"Come on," said Shifa.

The children crept quietly up to the boat and squeezed into the gap between it and its neighbor.

"I'll keep watch," she said quietly. "You go and check for the dagger."

Zheng leaned stealthily into Nathan's boat. He groped around in the dark, his fingers seeking out the box. The reassuring solidness of something wooden greeted him. He felt the grooves and ridges of a carving and knew it was the lotuses on the lid.

Suddenly there was a loud shout.

"Who's there?"

Shifa gasped. "That's Nathan's father," she whispered. "Hurry!"

Zheng snatched up the box but it was too late. A light shone down on them from a lamp held aloft by an old man.

"What are you doing?" he said. "Up to no good, I'm sure."

"Not at all," said Zheng quickly. "We were, er, looking for something."

"We're just leaving," said Shifa.

"It's Shifa, isn't it? Who's this boy?" said Nathan's father, bringing the lamp really close and making Zheng flinch from the heat. He turned toward the house. "Hey, Yasmin, come here and look at this."

A woman came bustling down to the beach. "What is it now?"

"Let's go," whispered Shifa.

"Not so fast, you two," said the woman, stopping the children in their tracks. "What were you doing? First our boat goes missing, then it's found abandoned in the ocean, and now you two are sneaking around here in the dark. All a bit suspicious, don't you think?"

"What's that?" said Nathan's father, pointing to the box in Zheng's hand.

Zheng promptly shoved it behind his back. "What's what?"

Shifa stepped in. "It's nothing. Just an old box of lace-making supplies I left there by accident. I wanted to come and get it before I get a scolding from my mother. We're going now."

"No, you're not," said Yasmin. "You're not going anywhere. First you steal my husband's boat; now you're trying to make off with something that's his."

A small crowd had gathered around them, lamps held aloft. There were shouts on the beach and more people came up to see what was going on.

"We didn't steal it!" said Shifa. "Nathan said that Razi could take the boat."

"Well, I don't see Razi here," said Yasmin.

"There they are!" came a voice. "The box is *mine*! I've been looking for it all over!"

Zheng was stunned. Marco! How did he get there? And making his way over with him, bold as brass, was Cook.

"He's lying," said Shifa. "These people are dangerous."

"Nonsense," said Marco. "As you can see, this boy is a liar." He grabbed the box but Zheng clung on to it like a leech.

"Give it up, boy!" Marco twisted Zheng's arm away from the box. Pain shot like fire down Zheng's arm and he flinched and dropped the box, straight into Marco's hands.

"Hey!" Yasmin cried. "You're hurting the boy."

Marco didn't care. He took the box victoriously and turned hurriedly to go.

"Stop him," yelled Shifa. "Tell him to show you what's in the box."

Marco pushed through the crowd faster at that, knocking Nathan's father to the ground.

The crowd gasped, and a group of people helped the old man to his feet while others surrounded Marco and Cook, stopping them from leaving.

Then came more shuffling on the beach, and more running footsteps. A curly-haired figure jostled into the crowd and swiped the box from Marco's hands. Marco roared but the figure squirmed away and ran down the beach.

Razi!

Shifa cried out with happiness, and she and Zheng ran quickly after her brother.

On the moonlit beach, Shifa launched herself at Razi. He hugged her to him, and then put out an arm to hug Zheng too. The three children clung to each other joyfully.

# Chapter Thirty-One

Razi felt like his heart would burst with relief and happiness.

But then they heard shouting and the sound of feet pounding across the sand toward them.

"They're coming!" cried Shifa. "Run!"

The three of them set off down the beach again, Zheng carrying the box under one arm.

"Where are we going?" asked Zheng.

"Not the hut," said Razi. "Anywhere else." The hut was the first place Marco would look for them now.

"This way," said Shifa, darting away from the beach near the reef and leading them through a vast coconut grove. They zigzagged through the wavy trunks at speed, with the lumbering Marco and Cook struggling to keep up in the moonlight. High above them, the ropeways of coconut-pluckers crisscrossed between the treetops.

Cook ran into a tree and knocked himself to the ground, then Marco tripped over his sprawling body. He cursed loudly as they untangled themselves.

This gave the children the opportunity they needed. They slipped behind an open outhouse. Oversized cooking pots sat empty on unlit stoves, ready for the process of turning coconut milk into oil the next day.

Zheng put the box down at their feet quietly and shook out his arm. The children leaned against the wall and caught their breath. The sweet scent of coconut oil came from the empty vats.

They waited until Marco and Cook stumbled straight past, still cursing. The children grinned at each other.

"I can't believe we're back together!" said Razi. "We were all in the middle of the sea last. Me inside a whale! I felt like I was in one of Zheng's stories."

Zheng guffawed loudly. "How did you get free?"

"I thought I saw Maalu spit you out," said Shifa.

"She did. If I hadn't been panicking so much, I'd have remembered that blue whales aren't physically able to swallow anything close to my size." Razi told them the rest of the story, shrugging as he explained how he'd fished Marco and Cook out of the sea. "I couldn't believe I'd had to leave you, Shifa. But somehow I had this unshakable feeling that you were alive."

"That's amazing," said Zheng. "Shifa said the same when we were on the islet. That she thought you were alive."

"You were on the islet?" Razi was flabbergasted. "How did you get there?"

"Oh, don't even ask," said Shifa. "We have no explanation."

Zheng snorted and sat down by the box. Shifa laughed with him. Seeing them, Razi began to laugh too, even though he had no idea what was so funny.

"It is amazing we're all alive now," grinned Razi.

"Thanks to each other," said Shifa, squatting down next to Zheng, "and with a bit of help from a certain whale."

Zheng lifted up the dagger. "And look who has the Dagger of Serendib now!"

Razi and Shifa grinned as Zheng turned it over in his hands, the lion's head gleaming in the moonlight.

"You know what?" said Zheng. "Right back at the beginning, you could have just left me to it. But you didn't. And I'll never forget that."

Shifa smiled. "I'm sorry I didn't trust you. You're right, you know. There is a great big world out there that I don't know about. I wish I'd been more like Razi and had some faith in what you were saying."

Razi shook his head. "And I'm going to be less blindly trusting! Seriously, if Shifa hadn't swapped the maps, I dread to think what would have happened to you. I would have never forgiven myself."

"It's over now," said Shifa soothingly. "We need to take the treasure to the authorities and then Marco and Cook will never get their hands on it."

"They shouldn't just get to walk away, though," said Zheng. "I want them to be caught red-handed. I want the world to know what they did. I want the captain to be recognized for what *he* did."

"How, though?" said Shifa.

A gleam of excitement danced in Razi's eyes. "We have something they want very badly. All we have to do is use it as bait to lead them on a wild goose chase and straight into the lion's mouth."

Shifa twisted her hair as she frowned. "How are we going to do that?"

"I've got an idea," said Razi, leaning forward, a grin slowly forming on his face. "And we have the whole night to make a plan…"

# Chapter Thirty-Two

Early the next morning Razi sneaked away to find a cart. After a night of plotting, it was time to set things in motion.

On the path outside a little house on the road to Galle, he had some luck. A carter had just finished loading a consignment of coconuts and was sitting by his cart, eating spicy chickpeas from a paper cone. The ox yoked to it looked fed up and tired, as if it were sick of life itself.

Razi sighed. It wasn't ideal but it would have to do.

He went up to the carter and smiled. "Hello, mister. Could I, er, borrow your cart for a bit?"

The man munched his food. "I'm just getting ready to use it myself. But you can hire it another time."

"I, er, I wasn't thinking of *hiring* it as such. I was thinking of just using it for a bit. Like, as a favor. I'd be so grateful. I'll load the coconuts for you."

The man looked at the cart. "I've already loaded them."

"I'll unload them then."

"Why would I want them unloaded?"

"So that I could, er, borrow the cart." That came out all wrong and Razi blushed.

The carter glared at him. Razi decided to be super polite. "I meant, I could unload them for you at your destination."

"A hundred miles away? Are you sure?"

"Oh no!" said Razi hastily. "I wouldn't be able to go quite that far. Do you have any other job I could do in return?"

"No," said the carter. He threw a handful of chickpeas into his mouth. Razi's stomach grumbled.

"Please. I really need it. The cart, I mean," he said hastily, as his stomach gave another growl. "Not your chickpeas."

The man considered Razi. "You're that boy, aren't you? The one who slapped Nalaka with a fish?"

Razi started. "Well, yes. But I-I don't think slapping is a good thing. I don't condone it or any—"

"Good for you," said the man. "He was rude. I knew your father. He was a good man."

"He was, thank you. He was the best."

"Are you trying to run away from someone?" The carter tipped the last of the chickpeas into his mouth.

"Yes. Two men who tried to kill me."

"What!" The carter scrunched up the paper and stared at him.

"They kidnapped my friend and tried to kill him too. They left my sister and me on an islet in the middle of the sea to drown in a storm. And they threw us out of our boat too, and I was almost eaten by a whale." Razi made his eyes go a little wider, to look innocent. He was hoping a little sympathy might get him the cart.

The carter looked at him narrowly. "Are you making this up?"

"No! I swear I'm not."

The carter looked up and down the path. "Okay," he said. "Take it."

"Take what?" asked Razi, hardly daring to hope.

"The cart. But bring it back in one piece within the hour."

"Oh, thank you!" Razi made to unload the coconuts but the carter looked annoyed at that so he changed his mind. What were a few coconuts, he thought. And they needed to get going. They were on a deadline.

Razi jumped on the cart and took the reins. He had very little experience driving oxcarts but how hard could it be?

Getting the ox to move turned out to be pretty easy. With a slow, plodding movement, the cart started grinding down the path back toward the beach.

# Chapter
# Thirty-Three

"Come on!" Razi yelled at Shifa and Zheng as they waited by the beach. He made sure not to go onto the soft sand where the wheels might get stuck but stayed on the hard path instead.

Shifa and Zheng came bolting up to the cart.

"What on earth?" said Shifa, stopping short. "What's with all the coconuts?"

Razi shrugged. "We can't have everything. I got a cart, didn't I?"

Zheng had already climbed in and

was pushing the coconuts around to make himself comfortable. He set down the treasure box and dragged a branch of coconuts over it to keep it hidden. "This reminds me of the time our crew got caught in—"

"Not now, Zheng," said Shifa, jumping into the cart. "Let's go!"

Razi moved off again, the ox plodding grumpily toward town.

"Where do you think we'll find Marco?" he said five minutes later. "It's so typical—he's always on our backs but when we're actually *looking* for him he's nowhere to be seen."

They rode on the main road, keeping within sight of the beach so that Marco would see them if he was still there.

And, sure enough, within minutes, Marco and Cook had materialized. They stood by the side of the beach road and glanced at the children coolly, as if they weren't bothered by the sight of them riding in a cart full of coconuts. The two men seemed to be deep in conversation with a woman from town.

Now that they'd been seen, Razi flicked the reins and the cart trundled away.

"It worked," said Zheng, looking smugly back at the

men. "They've stopped talking to that woman." As he watched, he saw the woman hurry away into Galle town.

"They're just waiting there," said Razi, slowing down. "Why aren't they following?"

"Just keep going," said Shifa as they turned onto a gravelly path lined with bushes with flaming red buds. "Or it'll look suspicious."

Razi kept on, rolling the cart toward the town but taking a slight detour to give Marco time to catch up. Whatever was going on?

They trotted on, keeping to the outskirts of town. The paths here were difficult, and the cart slowed down considerably.

"Okay, what now?" said Razi, coming to a halt near some wilderness where whistling spur fowl wandered underfoot. "Something's not right. Marco saw us. He knows we have the treasure. Why didn't they follow?"

"Maybe the woman was getting them a cart," said Shifa, crawling to the back and looking out through the greenery. "It's not like they can chase us on foot."

"I wouldn't rule it out, not with this ox," said Razi.

"Ha! I told you it was a rubbish cart!" said Shifa. "You admit it then."

"That's not what I said."

"You need to argue about this later," said Zheng. "Because I think Marco is coming."

Something was coming noisily down the path. Razi flicked the reins again and the ox hobbled forward, reluctant to move after its break.

With a squealing of wheels on the rutted ground, Marco erupted into view.

He was in a brand-new cart pulled by two sleek and strong-looking oxen. The body of the cart was black and shiny. Zheng looked sadly at their little coconut-thatched number with its tired, graying ox.

"Look at that!" shouted Shifa. "We have no chance now."

Razi looked back in dismay as Marco came straight at them, with Cook driving the cart. They were going to be made into fish food.

Marco's cart drew closer in all its polished, shining glory. Razi desperately urged their ox on. What had they been thinking with this crazy plan? They were miles away from town. No one was going to see them if they got caught and the Dagger of Serendib got stolen again.

It was a complete disaster.

And it was all of their own making.

# Chapter Thirty-Four

"This is terrible," said Shifa. "Step on it, Razi!"

"You know the ox *wants* to go faster," said Zheng. "Just try it. There was this time in the—"

"Oh, stop it, Zheng!" yelled Razi as they thudded over a bumpy patch and Razi flew up in the air before thudding back down in his seat again. Zheng hit his head and yelped.

Maybe Zheng had a point, though. Maybe the ox did want some excitement.

"Come on, friend," he said to the ox. "You can do it." He pulled the ropes and tried to coax the ox into going faster.

The ox seemed to agree with him because he immediately sped up. The *trot-trot* of his feet thudded on the road.

"Nice!" Razi whooped. "He likes it!"

And the ox sped up even more.

Razi leaned back, feeling the increased speed and coolness of the wind as the greenery on either side passed in a blur.

Razi turned back to look at Marco's cart. Cook looked determined and his face was contorted in concentration.

Their ox seemed much happier now. Gone was the glum expression of earlier. Here was a real adventure at last!

Razi managed to pull away, with Shifa and Zheng egging him on from the back. The treasure box bumped and bounced on the cart as they thundered on.

Razi leaned forward and urged their ox on even more, trying to widen the gap between their cart and the men's. The ox trotted up obligingly at once, kicking up dust from the road.

"Keep it up!" yelled Shifa, rattling from side to side. "It's working! Just five more minutes and we're there. And Marco still hasn't suspected a thing."

"*Go*, Razi!" said Zheng. "Beat him."

Razi grinned and waved a thumbs-up over his head.

Marco's cart edged closer, looming up behind them just yards away.

Razi pushed the ox again, gravel flying under the wheels. Cook had almost caught up now. They were so close. Razi's hands shook with the pressure and exhaustion. Cook's neck muscles were straining as he urged his oxen on, mouth set in focus. Razi was nearly standing up, encouraging their ox to go faster and faster. Cook pulled ahead slightly, but within moments Razi had sped up too. Dust was kicked up and the cart wheels ground along noisily.

But then Cook leveled with them.

Razi could kick himself. He should have kept to the middle of the road so the men couldn't overtake them. They were neck and neck now.

Then Cook swerved his cart against theirs.

Razi screamed as they slewed to the side and righted themselves again. Luckily the ox was unharmed, and kept on without pause.

"Stop it!" screamed Shifa. "You're going to hurt the animals!"

The men couldn't care less. Marco was roaring now, even slashing out at his oxen with a whip.

The three oxen lowed and hurtled on, sweating and toiling, locked in a race of their own. Then Razi noticed that the road narrowed dramatically just ahead, leaving only space for one cart to pass at a time.

"We're going to crash!" shouted Razi in alarm. "One of us has to slow down."

"Well, it's not going to be us!" cried Shifa, her hair whipping fiercely around her head and her jaw set and determined.

Zheng yelled from behind. "Yes, keep going, Razi!"

Marco's eyes were as wide as coconuts. The narrowing in the road came closer and closer. Shifa screamed, "*Stop if you want to live, Marco!*"

Razi was sweating profusely now but he wasn't about to give up. And neither were the men. Both carts hurtled onward at breakneck speed, a wall of rock on one side of the narrowing road and a large tree on the other. Razi held his breath…

Both carts took the narrowing at the same time. They thudded together violently and everything shook. Coconuts bounced everywhere, bumping over the children and falling onto the road. Still the oxen kept going and the carts pressed close together again. Branches scraped against the side of the children's cart, the thatching caved in, and some of it lifted off, the hot sun falling into their eyes. A horrible rasping noise told them Marco's fancy cart was scraping along the wall of rock and one of its wheels was wobbling unsteadily.

Then the road widened again and the oxen ramped up their speed, seemingly unconcerned about the damage to their carts. Marco's face was twisted in anger. He shook his fist at them and shouted, "Just you wait till I catch you! Enjoy your final moments!"

But Razi wasn't ready to give up yet. With a grunt and a spurt of effort he jerked ahead, and their ox thudded off as if its tail was on fire, leaving Marco and Cook sputtering and wiping the dust off their faces as the children disappeared from view.

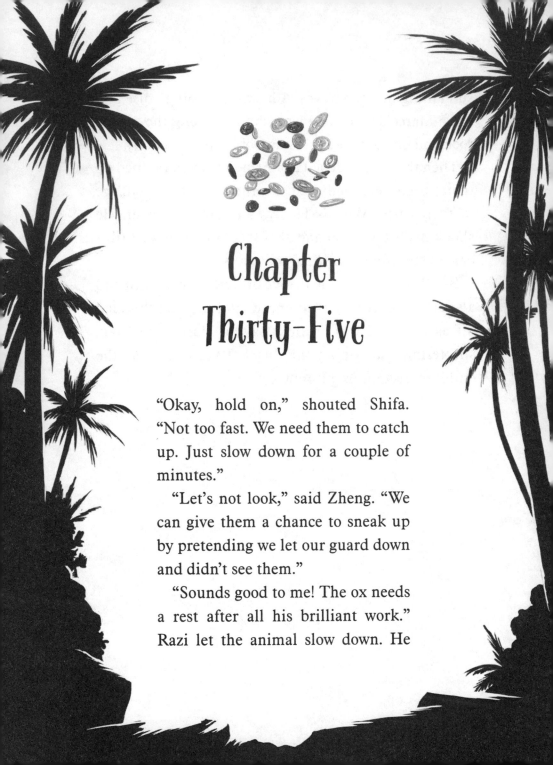

# Chapter Thirty-Five

"Okay, hold on," shouted Shifa. "Not too fast. We need them to catch up. Just slow down for a couple of minutes."

"Let's not look," said Zheng. "We can give them a chance to sneak up by pretending we let our guard down and didn't see them."

"Sounds good to me! The ox needs a rest after all his brilliant work." Razi let the animal slow down. He seemed much happier now, all lively and practically smiling after the excitement of the race.

Galle town loomed ahead, its narrow, cobbled streets in front of them. They trotted past the houses on either side—broad, airy verandas that came right down to the edge of the street and were held up by wide round pillars. The cobbles increased the pull on the ox and the cart began to slow down.

"Don't look now," said Razi, "but I think they're here."

He'd heard the sound of cart wheels behind them. There was a distinctive noise as the broken side dragged on the cobbles. It had to be them.

Gripping the reins tighter, Razi pushed the ox into a little more speed. He heard the wheels of the cart behind him speed up significantly in turn. He grinned sideway at Shifa. Marco was falling for it.

They passed a couple of tea shops, where men sat outside sipping cups of coriander tea and talking. They looked up curiously as the carts passed.

To Razi's irritation, they heard Marco's cart wheels slowing right down. He glanced at Shifa, who was twisting her hair again.

Zheng swore under his breath. "What are they doing now? We're so close," he whispered.

"Losing their nerve," said Razi, "is what they're doing. We're in the middle of town and they don't want to chance making a scene."

"Zheng, take out the box and make a show of looking at it," said Shifa. "Like you can't believe how beautiful it is and how much you love it. Just to give them a taste of what they're missing."

Razi grinned.

"What?" She glanced at Razi. "Too much?"

"No, no, I like it."

Zheng had the box out on his lap and had taken the lid off already, peering into the box lovingly. He sneaked a sideway glance at the cart behind.

Marco was pointing and shouting and gesticulating to Cook to go faster. The cart sped up again. It was working!

"Okay, we're on the home stretch," said Razi. They were going to pass through the empty market grounds and straight to where they were heading. He gently tightened the reins to signal to the ox to go faster. "We have to get them to race us again. They have to be chasing us hard so it'll be too late to slow down when they see where we're going."

"Zheng," said Shifa. "Pretend you just saw them and panic."

Zheng was all too ready for the theatrics. He gazed wistfully into the distance as the cart trundled on, then started and yelled as he spotted Marco's cart. "They're here! They're here!"

Shifa screamed too for good measure, and Razi pulled up, coaxing the ox to go faster.

Marco saw this and stepped on it too. His cart, battered though it was, still packed a lot of punch when it came to speed. It barreled its way toward Razi, wheels mounting over stray stones and bumping and swaying around crazily.

Razi pulled the reins to turn left at the statue of the queen. This set them on the wide path that led into the spacious circular compound of cobbled ground under the spreading areca nut tree, ringed with the houses of the village elders. This was their final destination. At this time, on this day, the village court was in session and packed with people, all ready to hear the criminal cases brought before the elders for judgment. Marco and Cook had no idea what awaited them.

Razi's cart flew down the path, with Marco pounding behind it. The drop-down gates of the compound were lifted and the way in was open in front of them.

Razi steered straight into the compound, the two men hot on his heels. He drove to the very middle of the startled crowd. Marco jumped down from the cart and ran to shut the gate. As he did so, he deliberately knocked the box out of Zheng's hands and it skittered to the ground.

Marco sprang out of his cart and ran to the shattered box.

Reaching the drop-down gate, Razi twisted the lever. The gate came grinding to the ground with a crash, cutting off any escape.

Marco, on his knees busily stuffing ancient coins into his pocket, jumped at the noise. It seemed to bring him to his senses and he stopped what he was doing and looked slowly around him. Clenched under one arm was the Dagger of Serendib.

Cook climbed down from the cart and stared in horror at the sight before him.

The village court, disturbed in the middle of trying a man accused of short-weighting a pound of fish, froze in shock. They stared at the scene in front of them, from the priceless dagger Marco was trying desperately to hide behind him, to the shower of coins falling from his pockets and pooling at his feet.

The men gazed back like mongooses caught in lamplights. All around them were accusing faces and pointing fingers, and an outraged muttering was starting to build. "Is that what I think it is?"

"How did *they* get hold of it?"

Marco looked at Zheng and Shifa standing by their cart and gazing solemnly at him. He looked behind him to where Razi was standing by the gate, trying—and failing—to keep a look of triumph from his face.

Marco's head dropped as he accepted defeat and the guards moved to arrest him and Cook. Justice was restored and the Dagger of Serendib was finally home.

# Chapter Thirty-Six

Razi vaulted over the fence and raced up the beach toward town. He ran all the way to the medicine man's, through cobbled streets, past groups of men sipping coriander tea and beautiful pillared villas.

Abdul Cader, the medicine man, was sitting at a bench outside, pounding amaranth leaves. "Your sister's inside," he said, nodding toward the door.

Shifa was mixing up a poultice as a boy sat talking to her.

Shifa smiled at Razi as he entered the room. He knew how much happier she was now that she could concentrate on her work here. "This is Vijay," she said to Razi. "He's an old patient of ours come to visit. All recovered now."

"Great." Razi smiled at Vijay. "I just came to drop off your lunch, Shifa. See you later."

With a wave, he took off again, this time to the lace mill and Mother.

Mother's workplace was a single-story building in the heart of Galle town, with pillars and windows all along its front.

Inside it was a hive of activity. The large courtyard was sunlit and humming with busyness, as twelve women sat at large frames making bobbin lace. Mother, working shorter hours once again, looked happier than she had for a long time.

She smiled as she saw Razi, kissing him on the forehead and ruffling his hair, looking for all the world like she had before Father had died. Razi gave her the money from his morning's sales.

"Thank you, Razi," she said. "Good day then?"

"Very good day. I brought some yellowfin tuna home for us. I have school for the next three days so that'll last us till next time I go out. Have you seen Zheng?"

"He came and said goodbye to me just now. I'll miss that boy."

"Your ears must be glad, though," said Razi cheekily. "A month is a long time to listen to all that talking."

Mother laughed. "Still, I really will miss him. Who else will tell me such stories?"

"Hopefully he'll come and visit in the future."

"I hope so. I'm so proud of what the three of you did, though you aged me fifty years in the process. I have to get back to my work now. Find Zheng; he said he'd be at the beach."

Razi made his way out of the building and ran down to the beach again. His feet sank into the hot sand as he sped toward the water.

"Hey, Razi," yelled a few children from his school as they ran down to the waves, passing a ball between them. "We're going for a swim. Coming?"

"In a minute. Just looking for someone."

"Razi!" Zheng was coming toward him, looking very smart and clean in a new outfit that Mother had made him.

"All ready to go?" said Razi, jogging toward him.

"Yes, it's goodbye to Serendib from me. For now. I've been to see Shifa and she said you'd just been by. Your mother has arranged for me to make the journey to the port. And from there, adventure awaits. Again."

Razi laughed. "As always. More monsters to discover. Villains to capture. Treasure to be found."

"Of course. And new friends to make." Zheng looked at the sea with so much hope and anticipation that Razi's heart lifted. He'd be okay, Zheng. He always found what he needed in the end.

"You know you'll always have us," said Razi. "Mother's really fond of you too."

Zheng nodded. "I know. I'll always have a home here now. Even Shifa likes me, which is the most unlikely thing that's ever happened to me." His eyes were damp as he turned away. "You're sure you won't come with me?" he said over his shoulder.

Razi looked at the sea, and the stilts in the water. Father's stilt wasn't empty any longer. Life was busy, with his fishing and school and his family.

"Well?" said Zheng, watching him closely. "I know the pull of the sea is always there for you, even when you try to stay away from it."

"The sea is right here, where I am." Razi laughed. "I would love to see the places you have, and someday I will. But for now, I have a family I want to be with every day."

Zheng nodded as if he understood.

"And I have something that I love that I want to keep doing," said Razi.

Zheng smiled. "I understand. Me too."

"Here, this is for you," said Razi. He handed Zheng the object he'd been working on the whole time the boy had been staying with them. "It's to remind you of our little adventure."

Zheng held the little whale Razi had whittled. It was as perfect as Razi could make it, right down to the tiny clefts on its back.

Zheng looked up with tears in his eyes. "I'm so sorry for all the trouble I caused by landing here," he said. "You and Shifa, you helped me with food, you helped find the treasure, you risked death time and time again. For not much in return."

"I think national recognition for returning the Dagger of Serendib is a pretty big return!"

"Okay, there's that!" Zheng sniffed. "But still, I wish I could have given you as much as you have given me."

"Zheng," said Razi. "You gave me my life back."

Zheng hugged Razi and he hugged him back. It would be a while till he saw his brave, adventurous, tiring, and fanciful friend again.

"Goodbye, Razi." Zheng turned around and went up the beach, walking quickly toward town without looking back.

Razi set his face toward the ocean, where his splashing friends and the fishermen's stilts were silhouetted by the setting sun. A turtle was walking slowly down to the water's edge. Razi followed her and they both dived gracefully into the wide, glittering sea.

# Acknowledgments

I owe Maalu's weight in thanks to my editor, Kirsty Stansfield, for helping shape this story to its best form possible, scrubbing the barnacles off and polishing till it shone. To Rebecca, Sîan, Beth, Lauren, and all the team at Nosy Crow for their hard work on my books.

As always, Joanna Moult, for being the best agent possible and making the waters easier to navigate.

To David Dean and Nicola Theobald, for a cover that splashes off the page. Nicola's vision for the artwork and David's illustrations blew me away.

To all my writing friends, without whom I would have been a blubbering wreck. Especially Yasmin Rahman and Hana Tooke, and all of Stroops, Aubs, and Swaggers. Thank you also to the authors who've read and endorsed my books, including Gill Lewis, Sophie Anderson, Aisha Bushby, and Julie Pike for the cover quotes. The children's book community is a truly majestic beast, where kindness and generosity run deep.

No book is an islet. So to the booksellers, librarians, bloggers, and reviewers for the waves of love for both *Elephant* and *Whale*—thank you to every single one of you. A special mention to teachers for all you do to promote reading for pleasure in schools. I've loved seeing the children's *Elephant*-inspired writing, artwork, and displays. COVID may have struck but I'm looking forward to diving back into bookshop events and school visits one day soon.

To my not-so-little whalelings, Nuha and Sanaa. Oceans of love to you for always being proud and supportive, and for your insights as the first young people to see my stories.

And finally, to the readers of *The Girl Who Stole an Elephant*. Those of you who enjoyed it, recommended it, wrote to me, drew pictures, dressed up as Chaya, or waited eagerly for this book: you've kept me going, so here's a massive whale-shaped thank you to you.

Read on to discover another great adventure
set on the amazing island of Serendib!

"A rich and joyful adventure story for those who
enjoy daring escapades." —*School Library Journal*

"Lovers of animals and adventure are in
for an entertaining ride." —*Booklist*

# THE GIRL
# WHO STOLE
## an
# ELEPHANT

# Chapter One

Chaya looked at the bronze spear pointing at her neck.

"Stop right there," said the guard.

Chaya took a step back and held up her hands. The linen pouch under her blouse clinked. The chatter of the crowds floated up from the promenade below, where the King's annual feast was taking place.

"What are you doing here, girl?" The guard waved the spear at her. From below them, the melody of the veenas drifted up. The musical show was starting.

Chaya shrugged, the pouch pressing against her chest. She rubbed her palms down her skirt and tried to keep her voice level. "I'm just looking around."

Her voice brought two more guards to the top of the stone steps cut into the hill. This was how the royal palace was built—a network of buildings at the top of the mountain, every rock and ledge forming courtyards and pools for the royal household while they ruled from above.

"You're not allowed here," the guard said to Chaya. "You should be down below, enjoying the food and the festivities."

Not Chaya. She much preferred breaking into the Queen's rooms and stealing her jewels. There was a particularly nice blue sapphire in her pouch at that moment.

"Well?" The man jabbed his spear toward her. "What have you got to say for yourself?"

"I wanted to get a little closer to the palace. See what it's like. It looks so pretty from down there." She pointed in the direction of her village and made her face go all wistful.

The guard sighed. "Fine. Just make sure you don't do it again." He put his spear down. "Anything past the lion's entrance is strictly out-of-bounds to the public."

Chaya looked back and nodded meekly, as if noticing the giant lion statue for the first time, even though it could be seen from villages miles away. The stone stairway carved between the crouching lion's paws led into the complex of buildings that made up the inner palace.

"Come on now." The guard gripped her arm, making her wince. He pulled her to the cobbled walkway sloping downward and toward the celebrations below. "I don't want to see you here again."

The Queen's jewels jangled in her pouch. There were sapphires, tourmalines, and star rubies, set in heavy, shiny gold. How many jewels did one person need, anyway? And these were just the ones from the drawer in the rosewood table by the bed. Pity she'd had to leave so quickly when she heard voices outside the door. And then to be seen when she was halfway down to the promenade was just bad luck.

She shrugged herself free of the guard and set off, her arm stinging from where his fingers had pinched her.

In spite of everything Chaya found herself gasping at the view from up there. The kingdom of Serendib spread out around her as far as the eye could see, thick green forests and strips of silver rivers, with the King's City below and clusters of little villages beyond.

But she wasn't ready to leave yet. Chaya paused near a tamarind tree and pretended to look up at the monkeys on it. Dappled sunshine prickled her face as she looked at the guard out of the corner of her eye.

He had stopped walking but was still watching her. She heard him swear loudly. "What are you doing now? Get out, girl, before I come and give you a thrashing."

The sensible thing to do was to get out of there as fast as she could. But the Queen's rooms were calling out to her. It was as if she could hear their whisper, right there in the warm sun. The softness of the velvet rugs, the gauzy bed curtains dancing in the breeze, and the promise of more riches within the ebony and teak cabinets.

Suddenly a commotion came from above her, near the Queen's quarters. She heard shouting and the sound of people running.

Chaya thought back quickly. Had she forgotten to close the drawer in her rush?

She sneaked a quick look over her shoulder to see a figure running down the cobbled path behind her.

It really was time to get out.

Chaya carried on walking as casually as she could. Her heart hammered at the sounds behind her.

She was just passing under the stone lion when she heard a yell.

"Hey, you!"

Chaya sped up, her bare feet scorched by the cobbles.

"Hey! I need to talk to you, girl."

She had to get away fast or everything would be over. Her feet slapped harder on the path and her breath came out in puffs.

There was a scuffle of hurrying feet behind her.

Chaya hitched up her skirt and raced down the path. The sound of thundering feet chased her; heavy sandals pounding on cobbles.

She pulled up with a jolt when she saw a row of guards racing toward her from below. She turned and ran blindly sideway, springing up some steps into the Queen's prayer hall and threading through its granite columns. Spears clattered against columns as the guards tramped after her. She got to the far side of the hall and plunged down into the foliage, thrashing through it and down the steps into the formal gardens.

She found herself close to the promenade where the feast was taking place. The smell of frying sweetmeats meant the food tables were just around the corner.

Chaya skidded to a halt in front of two boys stuffing rice cakes down their shirts. They looked up in alarm at her sudden arrival and took off in different directions.

Leaping away from them, she pitched into a crowd of dancers and musicians. The revelers were oblivious to the unfolding drama, and cymbals clashed and bare-torsoed dancers jumped and twirled to the beat of drums. She ran through the band, clapping her hands over her ears to escape the shrill sounds of the swaying flutes.

"Stop her!" came a shout. *"Stop her!"* The dancers paused one by one, and some of the music petered out. People gawped, looking behind Chaya toward the guards chasing her. "The girl! *Stop the girl!"*

A man in the crowd lunged at Chaya but she slipped out of his grasp and ran toward the gates of the royal complex. Coconut-flower decorations tied along strings came crashing down as she ran through them, wrapping themselves around her like a trap. She tore them off and kept running.

Elephants from the temple stood on the lawn ahead of her, draped in their mirror-studded regalia, ready for the pageant later. In the middle of them stood the King's Grand Tusker himself, Ananda. He was wearing his special maroon and gold garments, and his tusks were massive and powerful up close.

Chaya ground to a stop on the grass and looked back. She was boxed in.

She sprinted up and ducked under the mighty bulk of Ananda, the world instantly going dark and dank. His mahout gave a shout and grabbed at her plait, yanking her head back, but she broke free and rolled out on the other side. She sprang up to see the mahout turn and yell at the guards thundering toward them, as some of the elephants had started to toss their heads alarmingly.

"Stop!" The mahout waved his arms at the guards. "The elephants are getting disturbed."

The guards slowed down and Chaya took her chance. She ran to the boundary and dashed out through the gates. She was free.

Skirting the city, she headed toward the patches of wilderness on the east side of the palace, the wind flying through her hair as she sprinted away.

When she got there she stopped and leaned against a tree, catching her breath. She peered through the wilderness and smiled.

She'd lost them.

Chaya shimmied up the tree, hands scratching against the rough bark. She settled herself in one of the high branches and picked out the coconut blossoms stuck in her hair. Lifting her linen pouch over her neck, she dropped the jewels into her lap. They sparkled in shards of bright blue, green, and pink against the gray of her skirt.

It had been a huge risk. Her boldest robbery to date. And yet she'd pulled it off.

She picked a jambu fruit from a branch nearby and

crunched into its juicy pink flesh, peering through the leaves at the royal compound in the distance.

It was pandemonium down there. The crowds were scattered and panicked, clusters of people moving in different directions. The King, standing out in his gold-encrusted waistcoat, had come down from the dais and was roaring at his staff. The Queen and her procession of ladies were being guided out of the promenade up to the palace. The mahouts on the green were trying desperately to calm their confused charges and stop them from running amok. In the middle of it all, Ananda lifted up his majestic head and trumpeted loudly into the blue, blue sky.

# Chapter Two

After going home for a quick change of clothes, Chaya hastened toward the edge of the village to see her friend, Neel. She picked her way through the paddy fields, turning back from time to time to check if she was being followed. Ahead of her was the carpenter's workshop where Neel worked, and beyond its waist-high walls she could see him bent over his work.

"Hey, Neel," she said, stepping into the smell of woodchips and polish.

Neel looked up and smiled, then bent down again to the square of teak he was working on.

Stacks of wood leaned against walls, and half-finished furniture was strewn all over the place. "You're back early, Chaya. I thought you would be at the feast for longer."

Chaya slipped onto a stool next to him. "I...had to leave a bit suddenly. You should have come, though. The feast was amazing."

She peered over the half walls. The surrounding area was deserted as usual, and only a soft breeze swept through the paddy, rustling the underside of the thatched roof.

"We have so many orders to finish. Master didn't want me to go." Neel worked his chisel into the wood, and brown shavings fell at his feet.

Chaya wondered what was happening at the royal palace at that moment. She'd lost them, but would they just give up? Surely they'd continue to look for her?

"Are you all right?" asked Neel.

"Me? Yeah. Of course." She pointed to the square of wood he was working on. "That looks different. All geometric patterns instead of the swirly designs you usually do."

"Oh, this is something we're making for one of the foreign merchants. There's a new spice merchant in town, and it looks like he's here for good. Their patterns are all like this. I had to use a ruler..."

Chaya zoned out as Neel talked. How long would the

King's men look for her? They wouldn't give up easily. Her head snapped back at a thwacking noise. But it was only a crow hopping along the top of the wall.

"Okay, Chaya, what's going on?" Neel put down the chisel and stared at her.

"What do you mean?"

"You're all jumpy. What's happened?"

"You're not going to like it."

"Tell me anyway."

"It's…the usual."

Neel sighed. "And what's it for this time?"

"It's Vijay, one of the boys at the river. He was attacked by a crocodile when he was swimming. I was there when it happened."

"Yes, you told me. What can you do for him now, though?" Neel blew on the piece of wood, puffing out a cloud of brown dust into the air.

Chaya rubbed her nose. "His family has been told of a medicine man that can fix him, and he might be able to walk again. But they need a lot of money very quickly. They have to hire a cart for the three-day journey, and then there's payment for the months of treatment, of course."

Neel shook his head. "I don't know if I should admire you or think you're completely mad."

"This time, you might be right to say mad."

"Why, what's different?"

"Like I said, they need a *lot* of money. I might have taken something…more valuable than usual."

Neel stared at her. "Which is?"

Chaya undid the pouch and the jewels spilled out. They clattered onto the intricate carving Neel was working on, lodging in various grooves. The sapphire shone the bluest of blues, but a sparkling pink ruby was a close second, with a silvery star shimmering inside it.

Neel shrank back as if he'd been stung. "Chaya, *what on earth?* Where did you get those from?"

She picked up the sapphire and held it to the light. "The Queen's bedside table."

Neel looked at the jewels and back at Chaya. "Please tell me you're joking."

"It's not so bad." Chaya put the sapphire back with the other jewels. Neel was always such a worrier, he made things seem worse than they were. "I don't think they recognized me."

"Wait a minute, *someone saw you?*"

"Calm down, Neel. I ran away. I'm safe."

"*Calm down?* This isn't like stealing a few coins here and there. This is the *King* we're talking about."

"Queen, actually." Neel glared at her, so she quickly

carried on. "Don't you want Vijay to get better? If he's not treated, he'll lose his leg. He'll *never* walk again. And anyway, there's someone else who could use some of it too."

"Who?"

"You."

"*Me?*"

"Your parents could have the money so you don't need to work. You're thirteen, Neel. You should come back to school."

"I've told you enough times. I'm fine. I don't need any charity."

"Just hear me out. Not just school, you could even learn Sanskrit and the sciences at the temple. You could have a better life."

"A better life? Or *your* life, you mean."

Chaya threw up her hands. "Fine. So I might have gone a bit too far, stealing from the Queen." She noticed Neel's expression. "Okay, a *lot* too far. But I had to find a lot of money, *right away,* while they can still treat Vijay." She gathered the jewels up into the pouch. "I need to get these to his family. They'll leave tonight."

"Wait, Chaya. Think. How's a poor farmer going to sell the Queen's jewels? And what happened? You said someone saw you."

She hoisted the pouch back over her neck. "Oh, it was just one of the guards. He chased me down to the promenade, and other people tried to get me too. It got a bit… manic. But I got away."

"So now they're *looking* for you?"

"Yes, maybe. Oh, no need to look so horrified! I'll give Vijay's mother one piece that she can sell on the journey, far away from here. I'm going to hide the rest at home."

"The King's men are probably searching the villages right now. Don't go *anywhere* with those things on you. We need to hide them at once."

"Hide them? Here?" Chaya's eyes swept around the room. High shelves lined the far wall of the workshop, filled with tools, pots of polish, and wooden trinkets. "Everything's so open. What about that box you showed me the other day? The one you made with the hidden compartment. You've still got it?"

"Yes. Yes, it's here somewhere." Neel went to the shelves and hunted through them. He brought down a small box carved with a two-headed bird carrying a snake in its claws. He opened the lid and lifted out a drawer, and after some fiddling about, unlocked a secret compartment at the bottom of the box.

Chaya emptied the jewels inside, first taking out a tiny cat's-eye pendant and leaving it aside. Scooping up some wood dust swept into a pile in the corner, she packed it in tightly with the jewels. Neel snapped everything shut and put the box back on a shelf among a few others.

"It's all right," he said, as if guessing what she was thinking. "The master takes these every three months to Galle, and he's only just been, so they're safe."

"Good. This'll blow over soon. I can get them back then." Chaya hoped that was true. She unpicked a few stitches in the hem of her skirt and pushed the cat's-eye pendant in. "I'll give this to Vijay's mother now."

"Fine, but go home straight after. I'll head into the city and see what the talk is. You'll be safe once you're home. Your father—" Neel stopped, looking troubled.

"What? What about Father?"

"Oh, Chaya. If they ever find out you took the jewels, your father will be in big trouble."

"But Father's only a minor official to the King. Why would they blame him?" But even as she said it, realization slowly dawned.

"He's the village headman! He knows the palace. Layout, access, that kind of thing. They'll think he set it up. They'll never believe a girl did this on her own. And you know what the King is like in a rage. He will have your father—" Neel's eyes darted away from Chaya. "Come on. You need to go home now."

Chaya followed Neel out, with a backward glance at the box on the shelf. The Queen's pendant brushed her ankle through her hem.

*Father.*

Had she unintentionally put him in danger?

Neel's unfinished sentence couldn't have been any clearer to her.

## About the Author

NIZRANA FAROOK was born
and raised in Colombo, Sri Lanka.
The beautiful landscapes of her
home country find their way into
the stories she writes. She graduated
from Bath Spa University with a
master's in writing for young people
and lives in England with her
husband and two daughters.
Follow her on Twitter @NizRite
and visit her on the web at
*NizranaFarook.com*